C000000989

TOMMY GUNN'S

1914

FIRSTBLOOD

JOHN HUGHES-WILSON

TOMMY GUNN'S
1914
FIRSTBLOOD

JOHN HUGHES-WILSON

MEREO
Cirencester

Mereo Books

1A The Wool Market Dyer Street Cirencester Gloucestershire GL7 2PR
An imprint of Memoirs Publishing www.mereobooks.com

'1914' First blood: 978-1-86151-277-2

First published in Great Britain in 2014
by Mereo Books, an imprint of Memoirs Publishing

The address for Memoirs Publishing Group Limited can be found at
www.memoirspublishing.com

The Memoirs Publishing Group Ltd Reg. No. 7834348

The Memoirs Publishing Group supports both The Forest Stewardship Council® (FSC®) and
the PEFC® leading international forest-certification organisations. Our books carrying both the
FSC label and the PEFC® and are printed on FSC®-certified paper. FSC® is the only
forest-certification scheme supported by the leading environmental organisations including
Greenpeace. Our paper procurement policy can be found at
www.memoirspublishing.com/environment

Typeset in Goudy 11/16pt
by Wiltshire Associates Publisher Services Ltd. Printed and bound in Great Britain by
Printondemand-Worldwide, Peterborough PE2 6XD

Meet T.O.M. Gunn, a young infantry lieutenant in the Sherwood Foresters, just back on leave from India as Europe catches fire in the chaotic summer of 1914.

The British Expeditionary Force is off to France, and Gunn is determined to join the war before it's over. He joins a hastily-formed mixed battalion of reservists, regular and territorial soldiers to find himself pitchforked into the mayhem of the battles of the Marne, the Aisne and then the long-drawn-out agony of Ypres as the high hopes of summer sink into the frozen trenches of the winter of 1914.

By the time of the Christmas Truce with the Germans, Thaddeus Gunn and his men begin to realise that this is going to be a long war – and they will be lucky to survive.

About the author

John Hughes-Wilson, one of Britain's leading military historians, served in the army for 31 years in the infantry, the Intelligence Corps and Special Forces. He retired as a colonel advising NATO's diplomatic staff. He has been a regular live TV broadcaster for the BBC at military events and is the author of several highly-acclaimed works of military and intelligence history, his latest being the Imperial War Museum's History of WW1 in 100 objects. He likes good pubs and interesting conversation and lives with Lynn and a small zoo in Turkish North Cyprus.

Contents

Prologue - Nottingham, 2014

PROLOGUE
Nottingham, 2014

My name is Charles Gunn. I am getting to be an old man now.

The Gunn family of Nottingham have a reputation for living to be old and, God willing, I am happy to carry that on. Thanks to that, I have over the years been able to share the memories of my father and grandfather, when both were well into their seventies and eighties.

I was born in 1948 and my father died four years ago at 85. Before he died he left me a box of old papers that his father had left him. To be honest, at the time I just glanced through Granddad's battered old tin box; it was mostly letters and a few old notebooks, with the occasional insurance valuation for my grandmother's jewellery. I was still busy with the practice then.

However, since I retired last year, I have had time to do a lot of the things I had put off, and going through Granddad's box was one of them. I wish I'd done it sooner. It's a treasure trove. In that box were his diaries from his time in the First World War.

I knew the old boy had been a soldier, and when my father and I took him for a battlefield tour to the Western Front back in 1973 for his eightieth birthday, he talked quite a lot about his memories.

For example, that's when I found out that he'd been a soldier before the First World War. I never knew that. He never really talked about it. Up to then all I knew was that he'd come out of the army in 1919 and gone into business. But back then – remember, I was only twenty-five back in 1973 – I was more interested in the good food and wine on our French jolly than his reminiscences of the war as we trailed around a few old cemeteries and fields. What I did remember was that when we stayed in Rheims, the old boy rattled away in French; an old Frenchman came up and shook his hand, the waiters greeted him as an 'ancien combattant' and the manager brought us a complimentary bottle of champagne. I was impressed, but more by the free wine than by Grandpa.

I was wrong. I should have listened more closely. The notebooks are the personal diaries of the four years between 1914 and 1918 that changed his life. These little dog-eared notebooks make extraordinary reading. Sometimes they are just sketchy jottings; sometimes he rambles; sometimes, like the first one in India, there are whole pages of detailed writing. The little books are dirty and in some places almost indecipherable because of what I assume was mud and rain. There's even what looks like a bloodstain on the 1916 diary. I never thought of the old boy as a hero, but to this retired provincial solicitor, he certainly comes across as one. He had obviously lived through some incredible experiences - and I never knew.

Until I read them I never even realised that he had been wounded. But once you start reading the notebooks they are riveting. I sat in the attic for a whole afternoon one rainy day reading them until my wife got worried as it got dark and had to shout up to see if I was all right.

I have tried to get them published as a diary, but the publishers all say the same thing: the diaries are too scrappy to make a decent book. I was going to give them to the Imperial War Museum, but my son said that I should try and make a narrative of them for the family first. That's how this whole thing started; as a family history.

So I have taken the liberty of trying to draft his jottings as a real story and, by using his notes, try to make his memories and notes come to life. My wife thinks I am potty, but my son says it's the best memorial I can make for what was an extraordinary man and an extraordinary tale.

I agree with my son. And I hope that, wherever he is now, old Thaddeus Gunn, my late and much missed grandfather, agrees, and approves of my efforts to bring his amazing story to life and recreate his world of a hundred years ago.

This is his story.

CHAPTER 1

THE NORTH WEST FRONTIER, 1912

Young Thaddeus Gunn was lost.

Sent into the hills of the North West Frontier with a platoon of fifty men – well, forty-two, because of the sick, to be accurate - and no map, he had somehow taken a wrong turn climbing up the narrow pass deep in the mountains.

His orders that morning from the battalion commander of the Mohmand Field Force had been quite clear: *'To cover the flank of the punitive expedition by establishing a picquet on the top of Hill 724 and prevent any tribesmen from escaping to the east.'* The colonel's moustache had positively bristled as he stared at Thaddeus. The Staffords were short of men and having an alien platoon of Sherwood Foresters wished upon them for the expedition rankled, obviously.

'Think you can manage that, boy?'

This punitive expedition was certainly punishing

someone, Gunn thought as he mopped the sweat off his face. Now, as he struggled to remember his orders, an echo of distant gunfire echoed off the rock walls on either side. Somewhere far off, the rest of the expedition was involved in a real fight. He stopped, and the column of khaki-uniformed sweating soldiers behind him cannoned into each other and then halted. A few muffled curses floated in the baking heat. Some of the men looked nervously up at the cliffs above; most looked at their officer.

Lieutenant T.O.M. Gunn was as pink and sweating as any of his men. Laden with a Sam Browne sword belt on his left, a matching brown leather pistol holster on his right hip, water bottle and binoculars, all covered in fine dust, Gunn looked a very hot and dusty warrior indeed. He pushed his solar topee back on his head and pushed his wet dark hair back. He checked his new wristwatch. They were behind time, that was for sure.

'What now, sir?' Serjeant Dyer's pink and perspiring face was a picture of anxiety. 'I can't see no 'ill.'

Nor could Gunn. He needed time to think. 'Get the men spaced out, Sarn't Dyer,' he snapped. 'They're too bunched.'

He turned away to look at the landscape. Where the hell were they? The platoon was a ribbon of khaki at the bottom of what seemed a natural crack in the rocks. Behind them it wound down to the dusty plain where they had started from two hours before. Ahead it sloped upwards to disappear into what looked like an even narrower pass. The sound of another distant volley of shots rolled round the mountains. He couldn't see any green-topped hill. Everyone was looking at him. He came to a decision.

'Right. Corporal Keaton!'

'Yessir!'

'Take your section and scout ahead. Stay spaced out and alert. The rest of the platoon will follow a hundred yards behind. Go carefully and stop if you see anything.'

Keaton collected his section and they moved cautiously into the narrow opening between the cliffs, rifles at the ready. Gunn followed with the platoon and watched as Keaton's men merged into the gloom of the sunless little canyon. Nothing happened and they all moved deeper into the pass, which was sloping upwards more steeply now. Gunn was acutely conscious that some of Keaton's section had turned a corner in the rocks and were lost to view. The sound of far-off shooting was louder.

Suddenly up ahead, much closer, a volley of shots rang out. One of Keaton's men spun like a top, then dropped to the ground. Keaton's voice bellowed a fire order and a dozen Lee Enfields replied, firing back at some distant invisible assailant.

'Wait here, Sarn't Dyer!' Gunn shouted, as he sprinted forward to see what was going on.

As he rounded the corner the picture became clear; Keaton's men were stopped, lying prone on the floor of the little canyon, scattered behind what cover they could find. The soldiers were firing steadily towards a wide opening at the skyline crest of the pass three hundred yards ahead. Gunn got a glimpse of a group of Pathan tribesmen moving and firing down at them. Bullets cracked overhead and ricocheted off the walls of the pass. Without thinking he sprinted across to Keaton, jammed hard up behind two fallen rocks. Slithering to a halt in a cloud of dust, the young officer tried to take stock. A tribesman's bullet cracked into the rock in front and sang off into space.

'Try a volley, Corporal Keaton!'

He stared at the far-off tribesmen's bobbing heads as Keaton barked his order and his section fired three simultaneous aimed shots. The roar of the volleys thundered off the walls of the pass and Gunn saw a running tribesman drop like a stone and the other heads withdraw.

That was when Gunn looked across at the far wall and noticed a crack. It was behind him, just on the corner of the pass. He must have run by it. It was about a yard wide, almost like a doorway, and seemed to slope upwards. If he could just get the platoon in there ...

'Cover me, Corporal Keaton.'

Gunn rose to his feet and sprinted hard for the corner of the pass as Keaton's men opened fire, aware that bullets were cracking all around him and raising spurts of dust at his feet. As he gained the cover of the rock wall a hammer blow threw him to the ground. Breathless, he sprawled in the dust and clutched his left shoulder. His hand came away bright red with blood.

Dazed and shocked, he examined his wound. He had been hit high on the shoulder. The shoulder strap of his uniform was ripped and, looking down, he could see a spreading red stain. Furious, he crawled round the corner to meet a worried Serjeant Dyer almost face to face.

'You all right, sir?' were his first words.

'No, I'm of course I'm not bloody all right!' snapped the

exasperated young officer. 'I'm hit. Get someone to look at it, and then get the men ready to move.'

Dyer looked startled but complied readily enough. A couple of kneeling soldiers gawped at their officer. The platoon medical orderly came forward and began to rip Gunn's uniform open.

'Coo. You got a nice one there, sir. Looks like a ricochet, I reckon. Gone in sideways. Does it hurt?'

'Of course it bloody hurts, you idiot.' The medical orderly's name was Lewis, Gunn remembered. He calmed down. Lewis was a mainstay of the battalion hockey team. He was a good man.

''Can you stop it bleeding, Lewis?'

'Not a problem, sir.' Lewis was busy packing a pad of cotton into the arm, which quickly went from white to pink to red. He spoke calmly. 'Nasty wound though, sir. I reckon it's still in there.' He looked again and produced a little brown bottle from his red cross haversack. 'Ready for the iodine sir?'

'Get on with it, there's a good fellow.'

Gunn wasn't ready for the iodine, which stung like liquid fire ants, but with the eyes of the platoon upon him he bore the agony stoically enough as Lewis fashioned a clumsy sling and helped him to his feet. Someone gave him a drink of water, which was wrong, because they were all on strict water discipline, but Gunn was past caring.

'You all right to go on, sir?' Serjeant Dyer's concern was unfeigned. He didn't want to take over, that was plain. Only yesterday he'd been talking of his pension, Gunn recalled, and his little house in Mansfield.

Gunn moved his arm. It was numb and heavy. A soldier said, 'You all right sir?' Gunn shrugged them off and addressed the platoon, now bunched to hear his words.

'Listen to me. Corporal Keaton's men are holding the rebels off. There's what looks like a path just round this bend. Follow me and move quickly. We're going to try and outflank them and take them by surprise. Now, come on, single file. Let's go!'

With that he twisted round the corner and pulled himself into the opening in the rock wall. His head was swimming from the heat and loss of blood and he was dreadfully thirsty, but somehow Gunn forced himself up what looked like a narrow goat track that wound up increasingly steeply. He stumbled on regardless. With every step the pain was gradually asserting itself in his shoulder. He hadn't the faintest idea where he was headed.

Gradually the rock walls dropped away and he emerged onto a dusty little hilltop dotted with wild thyme bushes. It was a little flat plain, like being on the top of the world. A blessed wind blew, raising puffs of dust. The sky above was wide and blue. Across the valley a round-topped hill with well-watered green fields looked uncomfortably like the hill he suspected was his true objective. A startled wild goat leapt over the crest and disappeared below, dust flying up from its hooves. Behind him he could hear Serjeant Dyer ordering the platoon to fan out.

As he looked down from the crest line he saw a sight to delight any infantry soldier. From above, it was like a panorama. There, straight in front and five hundred feet below, lay the Afghan village. A thin firing line of ragged turbanned tribesmen was off to his left, busy shooting into a narrow opening in the rocks, their backs towards him. They must be the ones keeping Corporal Keaton pinned down. Below him he could see boys scurrying forward carrying bullets and water to the rebels from the mud buildings; the village – the expedition's objective - straggled off to his right. Far off down the hill he could see the smoke and hear the firing as the main force tried to assault the main entrance to the village two thousand yards below. For an infantry officer it was the chance of a lifetime.

He lined the platoon up on the crest line and walked the line until he was sure every man was in position. He spoke sharply to Private Evans, who was drinking from his water bottle, and to Private Thompson. who was settling down for a nap. Gunn was dizzy with the wound, the heat and the excitement. He warned Dyer with five men to 'watch the back door' as he put it, indicating the goat track that had brought them to the top. He pulled his Webley .380 pistol out, then realised that at this range it was pointless. And as for that stupid sword ... Then, with sights set at 800 yards, Gunn ordered his soldiers to do what they were trained to do: fire a volley, as crisp and disciplined as any at Waterloo nine decades before.

Thirty well-aimed .303 rounds from behind and above, especially fired by professional British infantrymen who shot for their pay, ripped havoc into the line of tribesmen below. Many slumped; the rest looked round startled and ran. A second volley added to the chaos. Gunn's head swam as he saw the tribesmen break and flee from the scourge. He was aware of Serjeant Dyer looking at him, concerned.

'Well done, sir. You got 'em on the run!

Gunn's head was dizzy. 'Ten rounds, in your own time, go on,' he shouted to his soldiers and then the world turned black and he fell.

* * *

There are only two of Gunn's Indian diaries. One is well written in a good fair hand and talks of his time with the 1st Battalion of the Sherwood Foresters and his experiences at Bombay in 1912. He makes much of his experiences in the officers' mess and from his tone he is obviously part amazed and part appalled at his soldiers, mainly Nottingham and Derbyshire ex-farmhands and miners. It is quite clear that his soldiers meant everything to him, despite their rough and ready behaviour and language.

The second diary is much more fragmentary and describes his experiences of being part of a detached company of Foresters temporarily seconded to a brigade on the frontier to reinforce a punitive expedition against rebel Pathan tribesmen in the hot season of 1913. The operation obviously made a deep impression on him, despite his obvious success, and he records the deaths of two of his platoon, Privates

Mulvany and Lance Corporal Hitch, whose families he wrote to, with genuine sorrow. For his platoon's contribution – albeit accidental – to the capture of the Pathan village, Gunn was Mentioned in Despatches, and later invited to a Viceroy's levée; a rare honour for a young officer.

As a wounded officer he was sent to the base hospital at Deolali by train, where he spent two months before returning to the battalion at Bombay in December 1913. He obviously made his mark, because in January 1914 he was gazetted 'Brevet' captain, meaning that he could expect promotion when the next captain's vacancy appeared in his regiment, without waiting for seniority. From Bombay in April 1914 he was sent on furlough to England, arriving at Southampton on 2 June 1914, before going on to Nottingham to see his grandparents.

It was there on 4th August 1914, the day after war broke out, that he took a train to the Sherwood Foresters' regimental depot at Derby.

CHAPTER 2

WAR!

Gunn had been impatient to join the fight from the time he had read the news the day before, so the journey by the Midland Railway from Nottingham to Derby on the 5th of August 1914 must have had him chafing at any delay. By the time he had found his way to Normanton Barracks and hunted down the Adjutant, an old friend, his future was assured. He was not going back to rejoin the 1st Battalion in India, that was for certain.

* * *

The first person Gunn saw as he walked through the Normanton Barracks gates was Colour Serjeant Hill, standing watchfully at the Guardroom door. Gunn knew that Hill – a

1st Battalion man like himself - was back in England, but hadn't realised that he was now Depot Provost Serjeant, an important man in the closed world of the Regiment. Les Hill was a legend in the battalion and the scourge of slackers and the regimental ne'er-do-wells.

'Come to join the war then, have we? Welcome back.' The NCO saluted smartly.

Gunn grinned. He and Les Hill went back five years. It was the then Serjeant Hill who had saved him from disgrace after a drunken evening in the warrant officers' and serjeants' mess the first Christmas he had been in the regiment and quietly steered him back to the officers' mess. Nothing was said about the incident, but he knew that everyone in the battalion knew what had happened. Curiously, no one seemed to mind. On the contrary, the soldiers seemed to greet him with new respect and sideways grins. Only later did he discover that he had punched and laid out an unpopular serjeant in the serjeants' mess lavatories. He couldn't remember a thing about that evening. He'd been careful with the drink ever since.

Gunn looked around. The normally quiet barracks was seething with hundreds of men. The square – the sacred square! – was covered with blocks of men, all in civilian clothes. A line of men snaked off in the direction of the headquarters block where a harassed corporal was chivvying new arrivals into line. Someone was waving a straw hat to fan himself in the blazing heat.

'What on earth is going on, Colour? Who are all these people?'

Hill rocked on his heels and viewed the throng with a

mixture of disbelief and disapproval. 'Volunteers, sir. Begging to join up. Bloody hundreds of them. Civvies. Some reservists too, of course. But mainly civvies who want to do their bit.' He shook his head. 'Waste of time, if you ask me. It'll all be over by Christmas. Then what?'

Gunn wasn't so sure. The German Army had over a million men, that he did know. Nevertheless he kept his council, saying instead, 'Do you know where I can find the Adjutant? I'm back on furlough, so I ought to report.'

Hill pointed his stick at the officers' mess. 'Try the mess, sir. Just gone for lunch. Looked like he needed it too. Too bloody hot for my liking.'

'Worse in India, Colour.'

Hill laughed and saluted as Gunn made his way to the redbrick officers' mess, with its double doors and ivy at the entrance. Inside was mayhem. At least fifty men were in the anteroom talking, smoking, drinking. Some he recognised, some recognised him. A mess waiter brought him a glass of cool Bass, which seemed sensible on such a hot day. Hobbs, the adjutant, pushed through the crowd.

'What ho, old thing. Dear old Gunn. What brings you here? Wait. Let me guess: you want to cut short your leave, eh?' He grunted and jabbed a thumb over his shoulder. 'You and two dozen others, from the look of it.'

They both turned to eye the packed room. Gunn noticed that some of the lunchtime drinkers were quite old. 'Who on earth is that?' he asked indicating a bald, white-moustached man in a thick tweed suit, despite the sweltering heat.

'That my friend, is Brigadier General Hetherington. Last

saw action in 1889 in Afghanistan. Been retired since ninety-eight. Has a big farm up in Dovedale. Told the commanding officer this morning that he wanted to offer himself to the colours for duty.' Hobbs took a long pull at his beer. 'Derbyshire man. Second Battalion. Must be seventy if he's a day.'

'What about the rest?'

'Mixture. A few like you, on leave or furlough, reporting in. Some, like Dove-Meadows and Bartholomew, retired but still eligible for reserve duty.'

'Some like that chap there,' Hobbs indicated a skinny youth with toothbrush moustache, guffawing at some joke, 'Thinks he can just walk in because his father's the Lord Mayor. Redmayne. Little ass.'

After lunch they wandered through the milling crowds back to Hobbs' office. Hobbs chased the Chief Clerk out and offered Gunn a chair. 'Let me guess,' he said lighting a cigar and blowing smoke at the ceiling. 'You want orders for France?'

'Something like that.' Gunn cut his cigar and stared at Hobbs. 'By the time I rejoin the First Battalion back in India it'll be two months, assuming they're not sailing back from India already. At least.'

Hobbs shook his head. 'The First battalion stays out there. Or so I'm told.'

'Right. So I'd like orders for the Second battalion ...'

'No chance.' Hobbs cut him off. 'Their advance party is somewhere on the way to France even as we speak, and they've already got a full complement of officers, including six reserve officers waiting as a draft, ready to move.'

If Hobbs had known the dreadful casualties that would

befall the BEF's battalions at Mons, the Marne and Ypres during the next three months he would have despatched Gunn immediately to reinforce the second battalion's officers. But on 5th August 1914, all that was in the future. He shook his head decisively.

'No. The Second's got more than enough already. You'll just have to wait for orders from the War Office the same as everyone else, me included.'

'But dammit Hobbo, there must be some way I can get to the fighting. I can't just sit around the depot while the regiment's at war.'

'Why not? You might be jolly useful at the Depot. You could help knock all these damned volunteers into shape. You're a brevet captain, so you'd probably get a recruit company, with any luck. God knows, that's going to be a big enough challenge. Remember, you're not the only one who wants to get to France before the big battle is over.' Hobbs nodded at the door. 'Every little poop of a retired or reservist officer is out there giving me his big sob story. Just like you.'

Gunn stood up and paced the office. 'C'mon Hobbo. I'm not retired. I'm not a reservist. We're regulars. We've known each other for a long time. What about special duties? Working at HQ? Stuff like that. There must be a way to get to France.'

At that point the Chief Clerk came in. Hobbs looked up, annoyed. 'What is it, Mr Riley? I said I didn't want to be disturbed.'

The Chief Clerk thrust a telegram into Hobbs' hand. 'You'd best read this sir. Fourth battalion. War Office is insisting.'

Hobbs read the telegram, then read it again. He dropped his chin on his hand and stared down at the piece of paper. 'How many reserves – unplaced reserves – have we got at this moment?'

Riley pulled out a notebook. 'We've got 512 other ranks and 24 officers. Most of them seven year men. There'll be more tomorrow, I'm sure.'

'Officers?'

'Twenty four, as I said sir. No CO or senior major, twelve captains - more than enough for company duties - a quartermaster and a doctor, but only ten subalterns. We need more junior officers.'

'So how many militia men still left on the books?'

Two hundred and thirty-six, sir. Some of them old sweats; ex regulars.' Riley prided himself on his attention to detail.

'So it's two three six, plus five hundred and twelve. That's seven hundred and forty-eight men. Correct? We could do it.'

Riley nodded. 'In a couple of days, yes, we could.'

Hobbs nodded. 'Then tell the War office we need forty-eight hours – no make that seventy-two. But yes. And tell them that it's up to them to nominate a CO and a second in command. I'll brief the Commanding Officer when he gets back.'

Riley massaged his face. 'No company second in commands, sir? We'll be short.'

'No, dammit,' snorted Hobbs. 'They won't need company two i/cs in France. Just let's get this started and show the War House what an efficient lot we are.'

'Very good, sir,' said Riley impassively and closed the door.

Gunn had sat mystified as this conversation had gone on. When Riley left he broke in, 'What on earth was that about?'

Hobbs placed his cigar with exaggerated care in the ash tray and leaned forward across his desk. 'Do you remember the old Militia?'

'Of course. I thought that they'd been disbanded for these new-fangled Territorials?'

Hobbs nodded. 'Well, yes, they have. But you can't just get rid of something that's been around for centuries, just like that. The name goes back to 1132, for God's sake. No other regiment in the Army can say that. There's been a militia battalion of Foresters since 1775, long before the 45th and 95th Foot became Foresters. So we've been gradually running down the old Fourth Battalion. Last of the Militia. Big links with the counties. One of the last in the country, I think.'

He plumed cigar smoke at the ceiling. 'Now the War Office wants to see if we can suddenly raise a special battalion as a GHQ unit as quickly as possible. Ready for immediate service, if you please. Well, the old Fourth, plus some of these excess reservists, look like being up to strength by the weekend – if we want to declare it as ready for France. We can't send any of these Territorial fellows because they're all Home Service only. So, by building up the Fourth we could give the War House their special battalion for France. What do you say to that, eh?'

Gunn was taken aback. 'What do you mean?'

'Simple. You've come here to badger me to get to France. Well, here's your chance, old boy. We cross-post you to take over a platoon of the Fourth Battalion. You could be in France by the end of next week. Now, what do you say?'

And that was how the 4th (Militia) Battalion of the Sherwood Foresters (Special Reserve) sailed to France on 24th August 1914. Among them was a delighted Lieutenant (Brevet Captain) T.O.M. Gunn and his platoon of 50 Foresters, reservists, militiamen and volunteers. They travelled excited, delighted to be heading for the action.

Many would never return.

CHAPTER 3

THE FORESTERS
IN FRANCE

Thaddeus's papers show that he sailed from Newhaven for France aboard the SS *Invicta* on 25 August 1914, docking at Boulogne. From there he and the rest of the 857 men and 28 officers who made up 4 (Militia) Battalion Sherwood Foresters were transported by train to a railhead southeast of Paris at a place called Meaux, near the valley of the River Marne. The journey south took over five days.

Gunn's first reaction was relief at getting down off the train at last. He looked back at the soldiers pouring out of their '8 Chevaux, Hommes 40' goods wagons, stretching and cat-calling on the platform as they shouldered their kit and swung rifles on their shoulders. Many stood down on the track urinating and making obscene remarks. At least the officers had all been bundled into a carriage, albeit a third-class one. The adjutant and the Foresters' new commanding officer, Lt Colonel Sir Thomas Birkin, were standing at the station exit talking to a major with an armband inscribed 'RTO.' The major saluted and the colonel walked back to the assembled officers, clutching a piece of paper.

'Right, gentlemen. We have our orders. At last. The Transport officer tells me that the BEF has been in action and is on the march, pulling back to a concentration area about 15 miles to the East. We are to join them there'.

A muffled cheer went up from the officers. Birkin looked at them and smiled. In just a few short days their new commander had won the hearts of his officers with his good humour, fairness and enthusiasm to turn his motley collection of soldiers into 'the best damn' battalion in France.'

'The adjutant's got a map, which is more than I have,' he went on. 'But I've sent him to a shop across the road to buy up every tourist map he can get his hands on.' He pointed to the east. 'We're headed for a place called La Ferté sous Jouarre, on the River Marne. We're to become attached to 19 Brigade under a General Drummond. We will be under command for movement but take our orders direct from GHQ. Special reserve, whatever that means. And when we get to this Jouarre place there'll be tents and a meal, I'm told.'

Birkin cocked his bluff, weather-beaten face to one side. Not a tall man, he nonetheless exuded a forceful personality. He stroked his blunt moustache as he looked round at the officers, taking them in one by one. 'Gentlemen, we are going to war. This is the real thing. Tell the soldiers what I've told you and warn them that it's marching from now on. Shank's Pony. Ready to move in half an hour. You wanted to soldier? Well, now's your chance.'

The adjutant, Johnny Wybergh, reappeared clutching a bundle of maps and looking excited. 'I say, the Frenchie tells me there's been the most tremendous battle,' he began. 'They've stopped the Germans on the frontiers, somewhere out near Nancy, but there's another whole crowd of them coming south, apparently from Belgium. According to her, they've already captured Lille and burned whole towns in Belgium. And,' he added, 'She says that the British have fought a battle too, at a place called Le Cateau to the north.' He handed the maps to the colonel. 'They're mainly for bicycling tours but all they had, sir. Enough for every company, as well as battalion HQ. I say, do you think I should have bought a newspaper as well?'

Birkin eyed his breathless adjutant with a smile. 'I think that'd be a jolly good idea, Johnny.'

And that was how Gunn went to war: with an *'Environs de Paris'* Michelin cycling map, and briefing his soldiers in camp that evening on the latest news from a battered and dog-eared copy of *Le Matin* dated 31st August 1914. As the soldiers sat around in the dusk eating their hot stew and bread they discussed the morrow in hushed tones. The men of one of the work details that had put up the bell tents had talked of thousands of casualties and rumours that the BEF was going to be pulled out of the line because it had been so badly mauled. No one really knew for sure.

As Gunn went to sleep that night beneath the stars, full

of French wine and bully beef stew, he thought, 'What a strange war.'

* * *

The next few days were chaos. Orders came in to the battalion. First a despatch rider warned them to get ready to march. They all paraded in full marching order. That was countermanded by another order telling the battalion to stay put, but be at one hour's notice to move. More orders followed but nothing happened. On the second day Gunn said to his old friend the Quartermaster, 'What the hell is going on?'

Old Tom Harper laughed. Gunn had last seen him as the Regimental Serjeant Major of the 1st Battalion when he had joined in 1909. 'This is real war, lad. In South Africa we got orders and orders, and orders. Then more bloody orders. Old Colonel Jowett never used to move until a staff officer came down and started shouting!' He chuckled and poured himself a tot of whisky. 'Live and learn, young Gunn. Live and learn.'

The next few days tested everyone's patience. Some wounded men from the north were put in the bell tents in the next field. The Foresters' battalion doctor went over to see if he could assist and came back with grim news, which he passed on over dinner in the officers' mess tent.

'It's worse than we thought. There's been some sort of running battle all the way from Mons, up in Belgium. The French are on the run and the BEF is pulling back too, according to some of the guardsmen I spoke to. In a deuce of a hurry, apparently. One of the doctors told me that all sorts of kit been abandoned. The really bad news is that there's been a lot of casualties. A chap in the Black Watch said that they'd lost six officers for certain and that was three days ago.' He returned to attacking the tough chicken that the mess cook had acquired at exorbitant cost from some delighted French farmer. The chicken was putting up a spirited resistance.

The officers looked at each other in dismay. The senior major, Carstairs, voiced all their concerns. 'Doesn't sound too good.' He turned to the colonel. 'What do you make of it, colonel?'

Birkin swirled his wine. They might be camping in the middle of a French field eating chewy chicken, but at least there was some decent wine. 'Funny sort of campaign. Don't forget that in South Africa it all went wrong at the start.'

Carstairs nodded. That's true. Complete shambles.'

'It'll take time to settle down, gentlemen,' the colonel went on. 'Campaigning is ninety per cent boredom and ten per cent excitement, don't forget.' He looked down the tables at the faces shining in the lamplight, 'Our turn will come; of that I have no doubt.'

Next day the Foresters got their turn. A dusty R.E. despatch rider appeared and thrust an envelope at the adjutant. Johnny signed for it and then went into a huddle with Carstairs and the colonel. Within minutes the bugler was blowing full parade and the company commanders were told to get the men ready to march. Gunn's company commander, John Hedley, a lean, slightly highly-strung reservist, was beside himself with scarcely-repressed excitement.

'It's action, gentlemen,' he addressed his platoon

commanders and the serjeant major. 'Action at last. We're to march north and hold the river line. We're on the extreme left flank of the BEF and we're to cover the units withdrawing and make contact with the French on our left. Get your men ready to move. Full kit. Large packs on the transport wagons.'

The rest of the day passed in a blur as the battalion marched north west. The day was stifling hot and the further they marched the more they ran into the ebbing tide of war with its flotsam and jetsam of refugees, French cavalry retreating and even a party of lightly-wounded French soldiers who sprawled exhausted by the roadside watching with lacklustre eyes as the battalion marched past. In response to Johnny Wybergh's schoolboy French, they pointed back up the road and said that that the Boche were about ten miles ahead. The distant rumble of guns drew nearer as the march continued, until they ran into whole units of French infantry trudging past, exhausted, unshaven and covered with dust. They gesticulated behind them, shouting 'Boche!' as they stumbled by.

The noise of the guns grew louder, and as they topped a ridge overlooking a wide green valley in mid-afternoon, the battalion collectively jumped as a battery of French seventy-fives lined up behind an orchard off to their left fired together with an ear-splitting crack. The colonel stopped and rode over to speak to the gunners, then trotted briskly back to the Foresters lying under the shade of the roadside trees. He dismounted and spread a map against a tree trunk as the officers assembled to listen.

'Right gentlemen, we're as near as we can go. If we go down

this ridge to the river we lose the advantage of the high ground, so we're going to form a skirmish line on this ridge. This is where we stand. We can cover the river,' he gestured to the tree line and a river about half a mile below, 'perfectly well from up here.' He winced as the French 75s cracked again. 'The French gunners are from 20 Division. They're on the extreme right of Sixth Army, according to their major. Told to cover the bridge down there. They don't know where the next French division on our right is. We're going to extend to our right and see if there's any one out there.'

He looked at Captain Tailyour. 'That's a job for you Bobby. Take your D company and act as right flank guard. See if you can scout ahead out there and make contact with anyone out to our right. Not too far, mind!' The 75s cracked again and an excited subaltern exclaimed, 'I say! Look!' as half a dozen grey puffs suddenly mushroomed in the air above the trees below.

Birkin eyed them grimly. 'That will be German shrapnel, I suspect. What they call woolly bears. We are getting close, gentlemen. Now, one last thing. I want a platoon down there on the river to act as early warning. Which of you platoon commanders speaks French? Proper French mind, not Johnny's 'plume de ma tante' stuff.'

Gunn raised an arm. 'I do, colonel. Actually, I do have an aunt in Paris. Honestly'

This was greeted with a gust of laughter in which Birkin joined. 'Well, do you now, young Gunn? In that case you're just the chap. Get your platoon down to the river, set up some runners with Captain Hedley up here and let us know exactly what's going on down there. Try and find out from the

Frenchies what they think is happening. I want you to warn us if anything's happening to that bridge. And if you see any Germans, then shoot the buggers. Understood?'

Gunn marched his platoon down to the bridge. Looking back, he could see the rest of the battalion spreading out along the valley ridge above. The road was littered with the evidence of someone's hasty retreat: French képis, a torn tunic, a wine bottle, even a French rifle, lay discarded in the dust. Near the bridge he ordered the platoon to spread out in skirmish order and advanced cautiously to the tree line overlooking the south bank.

'What's the name of this river, anyway?' said his platoon serjeant, a lean Derbyshire ex-miner called Doughty.

Gunn hadn't worked Doughty out yet. He was different from the pre-war regular NCOs he'd known. It wasn't that he was disrespectful; on the contrary. It was just that he didn't seem to bother about what the men called bull. He was somehow more relaxed, less formal but at the same time more committed to being an efficient platoon serjeant. He always ensured that ammunition and rations were distributed promptly. The men liked him and he enjoyed an easy respect with the platoon corporals. Gunn knew Doughty had been a seven-year regular, then gone back down the pit. Now he was back again and as a serjeant. And a good one too. Odd.

He consulted his sweat-stained map of bicycle rides around Paris. 'The Morin, I think, Serjeant Doughty. But I'm not sure if it's the Petit or the Grand.'

Doughty looked puzzled.

'The big or the little. Petit, little.'

'Ah.' Doughty peered through the reeds. 'Looks big enough to me. Hello, hello. There's Frenchies down there. Look!' He pointed to the far bank across the sluggish brown water, slowly drifting along in the hot sun. 'By the far end of the bridge.'

Gunn peered through his field glasses. A small picquet of French infantry – to judge from their red trousers – were getting out of a ditch on the far side of the river and gathering on the road. About a dozen men, he reckoned. A French officer in a dark blue uniform was talking to them and then half of them began to cross the bridge, coming towards Gunn. He watched as they reached the bank about a hundred yards ahead, then lined up and pointed their rifles back across the river.

'Do we let them know we're here?' muttered Doughty. 'We don't want to get them shooting at us.'

'You're right, Sarn't Doughty. Get the platoon spread out. I'll go down and talk to them. Guard!'

This was addressed to a Forester sprawling by the base of a tree, looking back at the little road that wound back up to the crest behind them and chewing thoughtfully on a blade of grass.

'Yessir!' Private Guard jumped to his feet and buttoned his tunic.

'You come with me and we'll go and talk to these Frenchies. You may have a message to carry back to Captain Hedley.'

'Righty ho, sir,' said Guard, slinging his rifle.

The two men emerged from the tree line and walked slowly down the road. As they did the blue-coated French officer began to cross the bridge with the last French soldiers; one of them was checking some wires by the side of the bridge. Suddenly the officer saw them and waved hard, shouting, 'C'*est fermé! Trop tard!*'

'What's he on about? What's he saying, sir?'

'Never mind that, Guard. It's closed. This lot are nervous as cats. Look.' He waved towards the French soldiers lining the bank, who had turned round and were now pointing their rifles at them.

Gunn waved cheerfully to them. '*Anglais! Nous sommes Anglais!* What's going on?'

They walked down to the bridge. It turned out that the French officer was a captain of Engineers and he was planning to demolish the bridge. The soldiers were the bridge demolition guard. In response to Gunn's question as to whether all the French units were across, he gave a very Gallic shrug, saying, 'I have my orders.'

As he did so a line of shrapnel shells burst high above the river, although well off to the right. The Frenchman pulled a face. 'You see, the *sales Boches*, they are close now. Soon I have to blow.'

Gun began to scribble in his field notebook. When he had finished he thrust the note at Guard, saying, 'Take this back to Captain Hedley and then come straight back. All right?

The note read: 'At the Morin Bridge. 4.25 pm. French sapper officer planning to blow bridge in immediate future. Bridge held by section of 12 men from French Infantry Regt 26. No. 11 platoon in firing line 100 yards back from river covering bridge and approaches. No sign of enemy. Signed. T. O. M. Gunn, Lt. C Coy, 4 Foresters.'

He thrust it at Guard. 'Off you go now.'

Guard folded it carefully, saluted and set off back up the hill at a gentle trot. As he did so a shell thundered into the hillside with a huge black cloud of smoke, to be followed by five others spaced along the slope of the ridge.

The French captain pulled a face. 'Ah! Now we start. Come.' He led the way to a ditch by the bridge. Looking back, Gunn could see his soldiers' faces peering through the trees at him.

'Wait!' said the Frenchman and six more shells thundered into the river and the banks, this time much closer. When the smoke cleared the Frenchman gave Gunn a push. 'Go now, my dear friend. Get clear. But quickly.'

Gunn sprinted for the trees to be met by Serjeant Doughty. He had hardly started to speak when more shells crashed down, this time around the bridge. One raised a huge tower of water above the river. Everybody ducked. A voice said, 'Fish for supper then, boys?' and was rewarded with a nervous laugh.

'Never mind that,' shouted Gunn. 'Watch your front and await my orders.' A click of rifle bolts told him that the Foresters were ready for action. He looked at Doughty, who raised his eyebrows. Seconds later another salvo crashed down, this time landing near the platoon's tree line. Gunn heard a piece of shell casing as it whirred overhead.

'Wouldn't like to cop one of those,' muttered Doughty.

Suddenly he heard shouting from the French section. A horseman galloped into view on the far side of the river, then rode hard for the bridge. As he galloped across the French fired a volley and the horse and rider went down in the dust, the rider motionless, the horse kicking on its side in its death throes.

Through his binoculars Gunn could see that the rider was wearing khaki, not German field grey. 'Oh shit! It's one of ours. Hold on here, Sarn't Doughty' as he sprinted back to the bridge to tell them that they'd just shot a British cavalryman.

As he got there another half dozen cavalry appeared and he could see the French levelling their rifles in readiness for a volley. 'No! No! Stop! Stop!' he screamed. 'They are British.' The Frenchmen looked round at him and then at their Engineer officer. 'They are British,' shouted Gunn. 'Let them pass.'

The first rider trotted up nervously, his horse lathered with sweat. 'Who are you?' shouted Gunn. The cavalryman, who was wearing corporal's stripes, looked confused, dazed.

'Lomax, Corporal Lomax, B Squadron, 15th Hussars.' Gunn recognised the cap badge. 'Why did they shoot Bates? I only sent him ahead to check the bridge. See if it's clear.'

'The Frenchies are jumpy, Corporal.'

'I'm not bloody surprised, begging your pardon, sir. There's bloody thousands back there. Huns. Great blocks of them, all on the march'

'Where?'

Lomax waved an arm back up the road. 'About a mile or two back over the ridge. Coming this way. We're supposed to be the left flank guard for the BEF. Ran into some bicycle troops. With a machine gun. That's when we got broke up. Scattered. Captain Roland went down. I saw that. Poor old Roly. Such a gentleman. We had to make a dash for it.' He looked back at the seven other cavalrymen nervously wheeling their horses on the tree-lined road and staring back at the way they'd come. 'Just us,' he added to himself. 'Just us.' He shook his head in disbelief.

Gunn realised that Lomax was in shock. 'Best get your chaps over here pronto, Corporal. The French are going to blow the bridge.'

Lomax nodded dumbly and waved his little group forward.

'Go up the road and report to Captain Hedley. At the top of the hill. You should give our colonel a report.'

Lomax stared past him at the enemy bank. 'What about you, sir?'

'Don't you worry about us. We'll hold the bridge.'

Lomax looked back. 'I dunno sir. There was thousands of the buggers.' He trotted back to his dead trooper to take his rifle and effects before swinging back onto his horse and leading his little troop up the hill.

For the next half hour nothing happened. The Foresters lay in the shade of the trees a hundred yards back from the river line and the French party had taken cover in a ditch on the home bank. Everyone stared at the skyline to their front. The hot late summer afternoon stretched on. Dragonflies skittered above the river. Bees buzzed around them collecting pollen off the mallow and Gunn wondered absently if there was a hive close by. Any war seemed far away.

It was Sjt Doughty who broke the silence. 'Aye aye. Here we go.' He pointed to the crest of the ridge ahead, where a small party of horsemen appeared on the road. 'Cavalry, sir?'

Gunn scanned them through his glasses. 'No. More like a recce party. Or even a command group.' One of the horsed figures, some kind of officer on a white horse, was gesticulating and pointing direct at Gunn, or so it seemed to him.

The French party below suddenly became active. Two of

the soldiers ran on to the bridge and began trailing a thick black wire back to their little ditch. As they did so the crest line was suddenly swarming with hundreds of grey uniformed men advancing in open order on either side of the road down the slope towards Gunn and his platoon.

'Shit!' said an unseen voice.

'Hold your fire.' Gunn's voice was unnaturally loud in the silence. He waited, brain in a whirl. The masses of soldiers were a third of the way down the slope. At the top a column of Germans appeared marching over the crest straight down the road. 'Can someone count them?' he called "Front ranks only.'

'About two companies I reckon, sir,' said Doughty. 'About a couple of hundred, spread out. Hello. What's he up to?' He pointed to a French officer who was standing up in his ditch shouting up at them and waving his arms. '*Tirez! Tirez! Maintenant! Vite!*'

Gunn grunted. 'He wants us to open fire. Too soon. Let them get closer.'

Doughty nodded. 'Well, he's given the game away. Look.' A group of Germans knelt down and started shooting at the bridge. The shots sounded a ragged volley. The Frenchman disappeared and shortly afterwards a wisp of grey smoke began to drift onto the bridge. 'He's fired the fuse.'

But the Germans had seen it too and those closest to the bridge began to run. If they could rip the fuse out of the charges, then the battle would be lost. A Frenchman fired and a German fell, but a disciplined volley soon drove the French back into their little ditch. The fuse spluttered slowly forward on the bridge.

'They're gonna make it, sir,' said Doughty.

'No they're bloody well not,' said Gunn. 'Eleven platoon!' he roared. 'At three hundred yards. Ten rounds rapid. Fire!'

Three hundred bullets fired by thirty men trained to hit a bullseye at six hundred yards cut the Germans down like corn. Of the group sprinting for the bridge, only one survived. He came running on, only to be dropped by a second burst of fire. The surviving Germans had gone to ground and begun firing back at the tree line, skirmishing forward in quick dashes.

Gunn watched the skyline. He couldn't believe it. Despite the firing a column of German infantry was coming on, marching over the hill and straight down the road. As he watched, it became a solid block of marching men. Which to engage? The marching column, or the skirmishing line closing the bridge?

He was aware that Doughty was looking at him. The marching column was a target hard to resist. But the skirmishers were closer, and were the immediate danger. 'Concentrate on the targets nearest the bridge', he bellowed. 'In your own time, Go on!'

A ragged volley of shots greeted his command, followed by steady, accurate rifle fire from the Foresters. A German skirmisher was hit and twisted before falling. A couple of braver souls who got up to dash forward were dropped immediately. The Germans started to fire back and Gunn heard bullets smack into the trees around him. A few leaves drifted down, cut down by the returned fire. The grey smoke from the fuse crawled slowly nearer the middle of the bridge. Gunn realised that the marching column had halted and was beginning to deploy at the top of the ridge ahead. Time seemed to stand still as he watched fascinated while the crack and thump of rifle fire went on all around him.

Suddenly three things happened; in his excited state they seemed to him simultaneous. Six shells landed around the bridge and the Foresters' tree line, huge explosions of coal black smoke. The ground juddered under his stomach as he lay there, half deafened by the blasts. Clods of earth rained down and he saw shell fragments slicing into the turf and trees around, flensing the leaves to fall like a soft green rain.

At the same time a roar of rifle fire burst out from behind them from the ridge above.

Of course! The rest of the battalion up there could see the battle far better than he could from his worm's eye view down by the river. He watched fascinated as the concentrated rifle fire of a British infantry battalion shredded the column trying to deploy up ahead. It must be a thousand yards range at least, he reckoned. Unbelievable! White shrapnel shells burst over the column, dozens of them. Those French 75s back on the ridge behind him were firing full pelt.

Through his glasses Gunn saw the German column cut to ribbons. Men went down, men ran, men fell and the German officer on the white horse disappeared as his unit dissolved around him. More shrapnel burst above the column, which broke up, the men either dead or running back over the crest to escape the remorseless rain of bullets.

That was the moment when the third thing happened; the bridge exploded in a towering hot flash of red explosion followed by grey smoke. Huge stones were hurled high in the air. For a moment all firing stopped as the stones, turning end over end, thumped down all around them or raised massive splashes in the river. Somewhere a man screamed. The grey smoke drifted away slowly.

'Well, that's fooked it!' said an awed Derbyshire voice.

As the smoke, stinking of bad eggs, cleared, Gunn could see the bridge. Most of the right hand side of the old stone roadway and the parapet had gone, leaving a huge scar as if a giant had taken a huge bite out of the narrow bridge. But as he looked he realised that the left hand parapet was still intact, and so was a narrow strip of the roadway. Not much more than a foot or so wide, but still connecting bank to bank. A man could cross, even if a horse could not. The bridge had not been completely dropped. The river could still be crossed. Despite everything, the bridge still needed to be fought over.

Doughty and Gunn looked at each other. The distant rattle of rifle fire gradually grew sharper to their deafened ears. Gunn wondered how the French firing party had fared. He couldn't see them. Peering through the long grass all he could see was the bridge, still smoking slightly from the explosion.

Suddenly he was conscious that Private Guard had appeared, breathless and hatless. He flopped down beside the officer panting, 'Adjutant's compliments, sir, and you're to withdraw immediately. Get the platoon back. They'll cover you up the hill. As quick as you can, he said. The battalion's on the move.' He mopped his brow and tugged his tunic open. Doughty's eyebrows shot up, but he said nothing. 'Captain Hedley's company is rear guard and they'll wait for you.' Guard stopped. 'I think that's about it, sir.'

Gunn never forgot that withdrawal up the slope. He had walked behind the tree line to collect the platoon to find that Private Webster was lying face down, dead, a huge stone from the bridge pinning him to the ground, what remained of his head mercifully invisible under the stone. Private Thompson had disappeared completely. His mates had no idea. A huge smoking shell crater in the trees might have been a clue.

And Lance Corporal Widdowson was lying quietly, back against a tree, weeping as his hands clutched at his belly, which was slowly oozing dark blood through his tunic. Gunn ordered two of his men to help get him back, but Widdowson refused. 'I'd rather stay here with my rifle, if that's all the same to you, sir,' he said calmly, taking his hands away to reveal his stomach, now streaked with blood and looked down at the tiny purple hole in wonder. 'It don't look much, does it? But I'm a goner, and that's the end of it. I'll stay here and give you cover.'

Gunn argued with him, but Widdowson was adamant. Finally Gunn shook his hand wordlessly and gathered the platoon back from the trees. Sjt Doughty joined them and confirmed the head count. Three dead, or soon would be. Kearey the Irishman had a carved-open cheek and his tunic was covered in blood, but he was still walking – and talking, as only Kearey could. Everyone else seemed all right, if a bit shaken. Time to go.

Well spread out, and in short rushes, the platoon scattered and began to make its way up the hill. Bullets kicked up spurts of dust around them and Gunn felt something brush his arm. Overhead they could hear the fury of the French 75s firing in support and suddenly a roar of rifle fire from their own company on the ridge as they neared the crest. Gunn heard bullets cracking round him as he raced for the top, shouting to encourage his soldiers.

Panting and with legs like lead, he saw Kearey urging young Murphy on, then saw Murphy drop like a stone as a bullet took him down. Kearey cursed, ran back down the slope and dragged Murphy bodily over the crest to flop down in safety behind a bush, then rolled his fellow countryman over. He was dead. 'Tis no good,' Kearey observed sadly to the world in general. 'Poor Pat Murphy's away with the saints, that he is. And him owing me five shillings, too.'

Chest heaving, Gunn took stock. Kearey's cheek was sliced open as if by a knife and blood dripped onto his tunic. Gunn's, 'You'd better get that treated,' was met by a stolid, 'Sure, it's but a scratch, Sorr,' as one of his mates pressed a field dressing on his cheek. The rest of the platoon looked a ragged bunch, tunics undone, frightened and panting with exhaustion. But at least he'd got them back. His company commander, John Hedley, appeared. He looked relieved as he looked them over.

'I'm glad you're back. We're the rearguard now and we've got to move. Quickly. We're concentrating to the east. The French will hold the bridge – or what's left of it.' He stared at Kearey's blood-stained tunic and his face, then noticed Murphy's body, lifeless on the grass. 'He's dead!' he exclaimed. 'How many did you lose?'

Gunn looked at Doughty. 'Eight I think, Johnny.'

'Eight killed?' exclaimed Hedley, astonished. His voice was aggressive, shrill. 'You've lost eight of your platoon? How?'

Gunn felt his temper rising, but Serjeant Doughty's voice

brought him back to reality. The NCO ticked them off on his fingers. 'There's Webster, hit by a falling rock from the demolition. Thompson, unaccounted for. Corporal Widdowson, who's still down there. Fatal belly wound, sir. Murphy up here. And Sullivan, Trowell, Armstrong and Skinner didn't make it up the hill. That's eight, sir.' He paused, looking hard at his platoon commander. 'Plus Kearey and Wintle, wounded, although Kearey's staying with the platoon. I think that's about right, sir.'

Hedley looked stunned. 'That's a deuced bad show, Gunn. I'm surprised at you.'

Gunn was completely taken aback. His temper boiled over. 'What? Surprised at me? And how was I supposed to stop them? A stone from the bridge falling on one of my soldiers? Ask the bloody Germans not to fire at us? We're all bloody lucky, Johnny, to have made it back up that hill. Look at this,' and he pulled at his sleeve where a bullet had ripped it open. 'That's how close I came to stopping one. That's what happens. Men get killed!' He realised he was shouting. 'This is a war, not some play game manoeuvre on Salisbury Plain.'

The minute he spoke, he realised he had made a mistake. John Hedley was a decent, competent officer but he had always been a special reservist. All his experience was just that - the annual manoeuvres on Salisbury Plain. And he had never seen action – unlike Gunn - and he was acutely conscious of the fact. Drawing public attention to his company commander's inexperience was a mistake.

The soldiers were listening open-mouthed to their officers rowing in public. Hedley turned on his heel. 'Well, you won't be getting a recommendation for a C-in-C's mention in my report on *this* affair, Mr Gunn,' he said with icy dignity. 'A bad show. Get what's left of your men to fall in and rejoin the company, now. We've got a march to do.'

Gunn shook his head in disbelief. The French 75s fired again, this time at the half-blown bridge itself. He wondered what had happened to the little French detachment down there.

> This incident obviously made a very deep impression on Gunn. The carbon copy of his report carried up the hill by Private Guard is still in his notebook for the period, and his diary account of the deaths of his soldiers and the argument with Captain Hedley is covered in some detail. He records that three days later the Commanding Officer spoke to him, giving him an oblique warning not to rock the boat with his company commander.
>
> The next day 4 Foresters took part in the BEF's push north across the Marne. As they were the last battalion to advance (they moved on 9th September) they missed the fighting, until on the 16th of September they were ordered by GHQ to carry out special patrols on the German line forming along the line of the River Aisne.

CHAPTER 4

IMPASSE ON
THE AISNE

Gunn's next entries at this time are erratic and he misses some days. On the 16th September he wrote:

> We've moved to Fère, north of the Marne, by a series of easy marches. According to the rumour mill at battalion headquarters, the French are making a big counter-offensive all along the Marne and the Germans were retreating like mad. We certainly found evidence that they had gone in a hurry. Lots of burned-out cottages, German litter and hats all over the road, dead horses, and even a smashed-up field gun, broken and abandoned in a ditch. Private Guard dropped out to collect one of those German spiked helmets as a souvenir and was crimed by an irate Sjt Doughty!

After the bivouacs by the Marne our billets have varied from day to day. Sometimes we slept in fields under the stars. At Bruys on the 10th the battalion was lucky enough to take over a large estate. The soldiers slept in the barns and cottages and the officers took over the big house. Inside the place was shambles. According to an estate worker some Uhlans had taken over the place the week before – the French owners had long since fled south – and wrecked it before they retreated to the north east. Mirror glasses were smashed, furniture and beds wrecked. Someone had been even been taking potshots at the ceilings. Even the women's clothes had been dragged out of drawers and ripped up. The wine cellars had been completely looted and there were broken bottles everywhere, although the mess serjeant managed to rescue some that the Hun had overlooked. And as the Adjutant pointed out, if he'd rescued some for the officers, you can be damned sure he's sent the best bottles over to the RSM and the serjeants' mess!

The only thing that wasn't smashed up was the kitchen, so that night we messed together in the wrecked Grand Salon. As the light faded the candlelight lit up the room. Just like old times. First time all the officers had messed together properly since we detrained. The food was excellent – bouillon, real pork and chicken, not bully beef in its various guises for once – with fresh vegetables and potatoes, and even if the serjeants' mess had got the pick of the bottles, we drank some jolly good wine. There was no pudding but some terrific cheese – all from the Estate farm, we were told.

I asked Johnny Wybergh how we paid for all this, but he just smiled and said that Tom, the QM, gave the Frenchies a receipt for everything and that the Army Service Corps paid for it all when they came along later. Went to a real bed in what must have been one of the maids' rooms on the top floor and slept like a top.

PS to diary. Colonel says he wants me to act as official interpreter to the battalion from now on. Maybe I will find out what is really going on!

* * *

17th September 1914. Post arrived in the billets. First time the mail has caught up with us. Most of the soldiers pleased, but Cpl Armstrong worried that he hasn't heard from his wife. Kearey's face is healing quite well but he will have a terrible scar, I think.

Two letters from father and a card from Dorothy. Father has all the local Oxshott gossip; it seems that all three Denks brothers have gone off to enlist and old Denks is livid; 'who'll help me work the farm and get the harvest in now ?' he said when Father was treating his arm.

Father also says that thousands of men are flocking to enlist from all over the country. He says they are scared that it will all be over by Xmas. When I wrote back I told him that I am sure that this campaign is going to last a long time.

The weather has broken with a vengeance. Terrific rain and the battalion marched north east towards the Aisne. The boys are wet and grumbling. When I pointed out that they should be grateful as they had been moaning about the heat last week, Bullock - the platoon joker - shouted out, 'but me rifle will get rusty sir,' to roars of laughter.

They are good men. Despite the rain they are in good spirits, because we are advancing and the Hun is on the run. Next stop the Rhine?

* * *

Gunn's diary takes a grimmer turn over the next two weeks. The BEF had been stopped on the River Aisne and, despite a series of attacks and probes, the British were unable to push north as the Germans entrenched themselves on the heights overlooking the river and used their superior artillery to stop any advance. It was the first time the BEF had run into well-entrenched resistance and casualties began to mount. The Foresters were held back as the GHQ reserve at Braine well behind the lines; but on 20th September they were ordered to detach two companies, which were sent to the BEF's extreme left flank to advance and patrol across the Aisne to try and locate the German right flank. C Company was the left hand company, with orders to patrol forward at night and identify the German positions.

It was a mission that was to have serious consequences for both C Company and the war on the Western Front.

Gunn was wet, cold and tired. He had been turfed out of a comfortable billet at Braine five miles behind the line and with the rest of the company marched all afternoon in the pouring rain north west towards a place called Condé on the River Aisne. He knew this because the Colonel had briefed all the C and D company officers just before they set off at 2pm. D company had gone north towards Vailly and C north west to the river with strict orders.

Gunn felt a twinge of excitement as he trudged down the valley slope in the gathering dusk. He wondered if the excitement was because of the unusual nature of his task. They were to cross the river after dark and then advance cautiously north to see if there were any German defences so far west. The colonel explained why it had fallen to them: the cavalry couldn't do it because they couldn't cross the river. And the new-fangled aeroplanes of the Royal flying Corps couldn't fly because of the bad weather. 'So it's an infantry job to scout.' They were to 'observe and report - nothing more,' the colonel had stressed grimly. 'And make sure that you get the message back,' he had added, 'That's the most important thing.'

As the soaked platoon finally halted in the village by the river and piled into a barn for cover, Gunn went forward through the streets. A gloomy and very wet French sentry gave a half-hearted challenge from a shop doorway. On hearing Gunn's French he relaxed. Gunn's big problem was going to be getting across the river, and in response to his question on the state of the bridges he was startled to learn from the miserable Frenchman that all the bridges had been blown.

Gunn was nonplussed; how the hell was he supposed to get his platoon across the river? The sentry shrugged and muttered something about 'Lavalle's Boatyard' and when pressed further, waved his arm vaguely and said, 'Down by the river.'

Very conscious that the dusk was deepening, Gunn walked down the street heading for the river to see what he could of the situation. As he passed the village church he noticed that its doors were open. He stood in the porch for a minute listening to the rain drumming down and smelling the mixture of incense, dust and furniture polish that reminded him of churches back home. There was no one else about and the place seemed deserted. But the door to the church tower was open, he noticed, and he climbed the rickety ladder to the bell tower with the noise of his boots echoing in the empty church.

From the open balcony a hundred feet up, he had a grandstand view of the river and the rest of the village on the tree-covered far bank. Through his binoculars he could see that there was smoke coming from some of the houses, but no sign of movement or life in the deserted twilight landscape. Far off to the right he heard the distant rumble of occasional gunfire. Otherwise all was quiet. Of the Germans there was no sign.

Once back down on the street he moved cautiously down to the riverbank. The rain had softened now and a gust of wind made a rickety door bang. It was signed in sun-faded green '*P. Lavalle, Bateaux,*' and in the yard behind it were half a dozen upside down wooden rowing boats.

Delighted at his find, he began to retrace his steps. At the barn he was greeted by a cheerful and much dried-out platoon sitting on straw bales and drinking tea. His orderly, Belfield, an educated man who was only too happy to act as an officer's servant, thrust a steaming cup into his hand. After the cold rain it was just what he needed.

A plaintive voice in the semi-darkness said, 'Can we light a candle?' and Serjeant Doughty's voice rasped, 'No, you bloody well can't. No lights, no smoking. You lot'll have the place burned down around you.' There was a collective groan.

Doughty grinned and came over, 'Company commander was looking for you, sir. I told him you'd gone forward to do a bit of a recce.'

'Where is he now?'

Doughty shook his head. 'Dunno, sir. Gone back to check on the other platoons I think. He seemed surprised we hadn't crossed the river.'

Gunn felt a twinge of alarm. 'Bridge is down,' he explained. 'It's a boat job after dark.'

They were interrupted by a bustle in the doorway. Captain Hedley came in, shaking water from a soaking waterproof. 'Ah there you are, Gunn. Where on earth have you been swanning off to? Thought your platoon would be across by now. What's the holdup?' He took a steaming mug of tea which someone handed to him.

'Bridge is down, according to the French sentry. But I've located some boats. Soon as it's full dark we'll get across. There doesn't seem to be any sign of life on the other bank.'

Johnny Hedley nodded reluctantly. 'Sooner the better. Remember, your platoon is the advance guard, so to speak. Once you move out, I'll bring the rest of the company up here. Make it company HQ.' He savoured a mouthful of tea. 'Best make a start. It's dark enough to move now. Leave one man by the bridge and send the boats back once you're ashore. We'll use your rowers as runners. And for God's sake, be careful. We don't want to be stranded with half the company on the other side of the river. Off you go.' He waved a hand.

The platoon traipsed in silence through darkened streets to the boatyard. The rain had eased off, but a chill wind made their damp clothes feel cold. At the boatyard they had a nasty surprise. There were only four boats in good condition, and as Serjeant Doughty ruefully pointed out, 'Some bastards taken their bungs out!'

In the dark they groped and, sure enough, each of the upturned boats had had a plug removed from its bottom. Presumably to stop them being stolen, thought Gunn.

'What now, sir? Stuff them with rags?'

Gunn shook his head. 'Too risky.' He looked at the dark boathouse. 'I'll bet they're in there. Let's break the door down and look.'

A Forester's size 12 boot splintered the door off its hinges, to a muffled cheer from the platoon. 'Stop that noise!' hissed Gunn. 'We don't want the Huns to hear us.'

He and Doughty had just entered when an irate Johnny

Hedley loomed in the darkness. 'What the hell's going on here? Why isn't your platoon across by now, Gunn? What's the delay this time?'

'Boats aren't seaworthy. Owner's removed the bungs. They'll sink.'

Hedley swore. 'You're sure?'

'Yes. Belfield, show the company commander the boats. We were just looking to see if they're in here. The bungs.'

Hedley swore again.

'How will you find them?'

'We'll just have to risk a candle.'

Hedley burrowed in his small pack on his hip. 'I've got an electric flashlight. Here, let's look.'

The flat tin torch threw a feeble light on the interior of the boathouse. Oars, cleats, ropes and other boats were stacked neatly – but no boat bungs.

Hang on a sec,' muttered Doughty. 'What about there?' indicating a large wooden wardrobe in the corner farthest from the water.

'Locked,' said Hedley.

'We'll see about that,' replied Gunn as he took a soldier's bayonet and prised the lock off. Inside, by the torch's pale light, they saw a neat row of round wooden boat bungs.

It was the work of minutes to force the bungs into place and make sure that they were secure. 'Once they're wet they'll seat even firmer, sir' said Doughty as they quietly manhandled the first boat quietly into the water. Rowers were selected and Gunn clambered aboard with the first dozen men. The Aisne was calm and the crossing only took a couple of minutes before they bumped the far bank. Seizing a handful of grass to hold the boat steady, they scrambled ashore with much splashing and muffled curses.

Gunn spread them out in a little defensive perimeter as the rest of the platoon arrived out of the dark. He moved them fifty yards further ashore and waited by the bank for the other platoons to arrive. As they did so he met them and whispered orders that put 10 platoon to the right and 12 platoon to the left. The last boat brought Johnny Hedley. 'What's holding you up now?' he hissed. 'It's taken nearly two hours to get the company ashore.'

'We've all been as quick as we could,' countered Gunn.

'Well it's not bloody quick enough! Don't forget you're supposed to do your patrol and get back before dawn. And it's nearly eleven o'clock already.'

'In that case the sooner I get started the better,' retorted Gunn curtly and turned on his heel to fade into the darkness.

'Gunn! Gunn!' he heard Hedley call after him, but he ignored his clearly anxious and over-stressed company commander.

The patrol started as a slow, nerve-racking advance through the darkened village. As they left the houses behind, there was no sign of life whatsoever except for a barking dog in a deserted farmhouse by the roadside, howling in misery.

'I'll bet they've chained that'un oop,' muttered a Forester.

'Poor bugger'll probably starve,' replied another. 'Bastards.'

'Quiet!' hissed Gunn.

Cautiously, but with increasing confidence, they probed forward through a line of wood dark on the skyline. The river and Condé village were now a thousand yards behind them. As they topped the rise at the valley crest, Gunn made them lie down and in the pale moonlight they scanned the terrain ahead. Silence reigned. Far off to the north they could see some lights. Villages. Gunn remembered their names; Sancy and Nanteuil. 'If you end up there you'll have gone too far,' he recalled the CO's briefing.

He lay there wondering what to do next. The other platoons were somewhere far off to left and right and probably wondering what to do, just like him. Away to the right he could hear the far-off rumble of occasional artillery. No sign of the Germans; deserted villages; not a shot to be heard. Was he leading his platoon into an ambush in the dark?

'What next, sir? said Doughty quietly.

Gunn looked at his wristwatch. 'Gone midnight. What time's dawn?'

'Six. About six. We need to be back at the river four ack emma in that case? To be safe?'

'Agreed. Let's lie up here for a while and see what's going on. Then we can push on for a couple of hours. After that we pull back.'

Doughty grunted. 'I'll just go and check on the platoon,' he said and disappeared into the dark.

Gunn stared out over the moonlit landscape. Nothing moved. An owl hooted and far off he thought he could hear a train. He scanned the dark horizon and sure enough he could see silver in the moonlight, the steam of a train's exhaust heading right to left as he watched.

Doughty loomed out of the dark and lay beside him.

'All well, Sarn't Doughty?'

'Just caught two of the buggers asleep, sir. Bullock and Smith.'

'Oh, damn.' 'Falling asleep on sentry while on active service' was one of the most serious military offences, Gunn remembered. A capital offence. 'Did you charge them?'

'No point, sir. Just gave them a bloody good kick each. They'll stay awake in future.'

Gunn grinned in the darkness. He liked Doughty. 'Right,' he made his mind up. 'Get the men together and we'll probe ahead. But carefully.'

As the platoon gathered round he gave his orders in a low voice. 'Right. We're about a mile north of the river. There's no sign of the Germans, but that doesn't mean they're not here. So we are going to advance in single file up this road. Carefully. I'll lead; Serjeant Doughty will bring up the rear. If we see the Germans we just watch and count them. That will stop any accidents. No firing. Section commanders, I want every rifle to be checked to make sure that no one has got one up the spout. Then we will pull back to the river the way we came and get back across to report what we've seen to Captain Hedley. If anything goes wrong and we bump into the Germans or there's firing, then we get back to the river as fast as we can. There might be a roadblock or a sentry. Any questions?'

There were no questions, and Gunn led the platoon along the narrow country road. For a mile they walked cautiously forward, stopping every five minutes to listen. At three o'clock he gathered the platoon again and told them in a low voice what he had decided. 'Right. There's nothing as far as we can see. So what we're going to do is stop at the next ridge and then turn back.'

The platoon murmured assent and they crept cautiously forward towards the trees on the little ridge line a quarter of a mile ahead. As they moved the last hundred yards, Belfield whispered, 'What's that smell?'

Gunn stopped and sniffed. Belfield was right. There was a definite smell in the air. Horses? Livestock? Meat? Burning? He halted the platoon and went forward to peer into the little valley below. What he saw turned his stomach over.

The whole valley was crammed with Germans. In the moonlight he could see horses, wagons, dozens of tents and sentries patrolling. The remains of campfires glowed. As far as he looked to left and right there were Germans in their hundreds, no thousands, sleeping on the ground alongside a single railway line that ran across his front, its rails gleaming in the pale moonlight. Below him, a small station with a water tower had a light on and through his binoculars he could see German officers inside clustered round a map.

'Christ!' He pulled back from the crest and rolled on his back. Doughty appeared. 'What's up, sir?'

'Take a look.' Gunn gestured with his chin at the valley and handed the binoculars to the NCO.

Doughty inched forward. 'Shit!' He stared into the darkness. 'Well, we've certainly found them. There's thousands of the buggers. What are they doing?'

'Waiting for a train, that's what.'

Doughty thought for a minute. 'Yes, but which way?'

'That is the question, my friend. Have they just got off, or are they waiting to load?'

Doughty nodded. 'If they've just got off they'd be marching by now. They must be waiting for a train.'

'I agree. But which way are they headed? North or south?'

Doughty shook his head and stared down into the little valley. 'That's what they'll want to know, isn't it? Back at battalion.'

Gunn looked at his watch and came to a decision. 'I want you to lead the platoon back, Sarn't Doughty. Get back with what we've seen so far and I'll stay here and find out what this lot are up to and follow on later. All right?'

Doughty digested this in silence. 'How will you get back, sir? You're not thinking to cross the river in daylight?'

'I'll cross that bridge when I come to it.'

Doughty laughed.

Gunn grunted. 'Not quite what I meant to say. I think I'll need a couple of chaps to stay with me to make sure the message gets back. Belt and braces. Volunteers?'

Doughty nodded. 'I'll ask the lads.'

He disappeared in the dark to return a couple of minutes later to Gunn, still intently watching the German-filled valley. Gunn saw his teeth gleam in the dark. 'Problem?'

'Aye, you could say, sir. They all want to bloody stay.'

Gunn stared at him in amazement. '*All* of them?'

'All of them. Even Smith and Bullock.' Doughty grinned at his officer.

Gunn considered this new facet of his army career. His new soldiers – a strange mix of reservists, Militia volunteers, and returned old soldiers were unlike many of the regulars he had encountered in the past. A little older, better educated in many cases, more enthusiastic, uncomplaining and determined to press on. He shook his head. 'They're potty. The lot of them. Barmy. Very well. Tell Corporal Ruddock that his section stays with me – the rest go back with you. Now. Is that clear?'

'Yessir. How will you get back?'

'I don't know. But as soon as I've got the answer to this little lot we'll make our way back to the river bridge. We'll get back somehow. Ask Captain Hedley to detail someone to watch out for us at the river. Better take this note.' He fumbled in the dark for his Field Service Notebook and laboriously wrote out a message in capitals. Writing in the dark was not a skill he had mastered. He handed it to Doughty. 'Good luck, Sarn't Doughty. Look after the boys. Now off you go.'

Doughty hesitated and Gunn thought he was going to argue. Instead he stuck his hand out and to Gunn's intense surprise, shook his hand. 'Good luck to you, sir.'

When the platoon had gone, Corporal Ruddock closed up on him. Gunn showed him the valley full of Germans below. Ruddock's reaction was both unprintable and noisy. Gunn shushed him. 'Get your men in all round defence. Quietly now. We're staying here in the trees until we know where this lot is going, then we're getting back to the company. Don't make a noise and if the Germans start to come up the hill we withdraw – quietly. Got that?'

'Yessir.' Ruddock started at the valley. He shook his head in amazement. 'There must be hundreds of them. I'll warn the lads.'

The little group of a dozen soldiers lay quietly. Gunn checked his watch. And again. And again. By five o'clock the first shimmerings of dawn had appeared as the sky to the east lightened. Suddenly all was action in the valley below. A bugle sounded and men stood to arms. Officers appeared and paraded their men.

Ruddock clutched Gunn's arm. 'Look over there, sir,' he said, pointing to the right, where about ten Germans, rifles slung, were laboriously climbing up the steep valley side about four hundred yards away. Gunn watched with alarm. This was a picquet sent to do exactly what he would have done; set up a watching sentry group on the high ground to cover the main body of the troops below.

Stay on the ridge or move back? He eyed his line of retreat in the growing light. The nearest cover was a wood about a quarter of a mile away. If he moved back they risked being seen as they crossed the open fields behind.

'We stay,' he said firmly. Ruddock's eyebrows shot up, but he said nothing. 'Pull the men in a tight circle as close to me as possible, Corporal Ruddock. Quietly.' Gunn looked at the Germans toiling up the slope well off to their right. 'I reckon they'll occupy that clump of trees, there, further down the ridge and stay put to act as an observation post where they can see the road. We stay put too. They don't know we're here, but we know where they are. Leave it. No one can see us in this little copse unless they come looking.'

Ruddock nodded agreement. He was a farmer's boy, Ruddock remembered, from up Chesterfield way. Militia man. Small, hard, wiry, and could stalk like a cat. The men respected him.

As full daylight broke under a lowering sky of low cloud,

they stayed watching the valley. Nothing happened except for Ruddock pointing out some soldiers who had come a little way up the slope below them to relieve themselves, much to the suppressed mirth of the Foresters.

After about an hour the Germans in the valley suddenly sprang to life and became a hive of activity, striking tents, parading, clearing the ground and falling in by units.

'They're getting ready to move,' muttered Gunn. Sure enough, the German picquet to their right suddenly reappeared and began to stumble down the hill to rejoin their unit, and about ten minutes later a steam engine and a train of cattle trucks appeared off to their right. It slowly clanked to a halt at the little station below, steam bursting from every valve. As the engine took on water Gunn watched the Germans entrain; cavalry, artillery and solid blocks of infantry marching on board with officers and NCOs fussing around them. Then, with much heel-clicking and saluting, the last officers mounted the train's only carriage, and with a toot from the engine's whistle the train slowly began to chug its way off to their left – to the north west.

To his delight, Gunn could clearly see the chalked inscriptions on the sides of the carriages and wagons: '*Nach Flanderen!*'; '*77 Res Rgt Bayern; 'Art Grp 45;' 'Offizieren;' and 'Kav Hussaren 14.*' He copied them all down carefully in his book and, with Ruddock's help, counted the trucks, which seemed to go on for ever.

'Sixty-eight it is, sir,' the corporal announced proudly as the last truck disappeared from view. 'They've gone.'

'Can I take a piss now, corp?' said a plaintive voice to

muffled laughter, as the now empty valley settled back to silence.

Gunn smiled. 'Yes. All of you, we can relax a little now. Corporal Ruddock, spread your boys out again to the corners of the trees. Watch out behind us, particularly. I can watch the valley. Half of you get a brew going here in the middle.'

'Are we not going back now, sir?' said a voice.

Gunn shook his head decisively. 'No. We wait till dark.'

The Foresters looked at each other. 'You mean we stay here all day?' said another.

'Exactly. So post sentries, get some snap down your necks, start on your iron ration, and then the rest of you get some sleep. We'll wait till it's dark and safe.'

The soldiers accepted his decision and settled down for the day. Someone brought Gunn a mug of tea with the muttered joke, 'But no rum ration this morning, sir.'

Gunn was glad he had decided to wait. At exactly 17 minutes past the hour another long troop train rolled by heading north, and two hours later another, again at 17 minutes past the hour. Trust the Germans, thought Gunn as he counted the trucks. Systematic as ever. Both trains were packed with troops.

Later in the day another train came in and stopped at the station for the engine to take on water. Hundreds of grey-clad soldiers got out, stretching their legs and relieving themselves. After ten minutes they mounted up and the train lumbered off to the north. Gunn catnapped as the afternoon wore on, but despite Corporal Ruddock's, 'I'll take the stag for the next three hours, sir,' he couldn't sleep.

As the sun set below the low clouds another train clanked slowly by, packed with flatbed trucks carrying artillery pieces and limbers. Excited, Gunn counted them all. Thirty-two guns and all their wagons - an artillery battalion or regiment, surely. All headed north west.

As the light faded they stood to and watched the valley. The only thing they saw was a small deer, which suddenly appeared and nervously drank from the puddle at the bottom of the water tower before bolting in panic at some unheard alarm. By nine o'clock it was pitch dark and Ruddock sent a couple of his men down to refill their water bottles from the railway water tower. They came back half soaked, but giggling like schoolboys up to mischief.

Gunn assembled his little group, warning them that they were to stay together but, if they did get split up, to make for the riverbank by the bridge. He added, 'and if I don't get through Corporal Ruddock has got a copy of all the intelligence we've gathered. Just in case.'

They set off to the south, retracing their steps and cautious as cats. Once something shot across in front of them in the darkness and they all froze, but whatever it was disappeared and they relaxed, hearts pounding. 'Probably another deer, sir,' whispered Ruddock.

It took the group three hours to retrace their steps. Far off to their left an occasional flash and a sound like a door slamming told them that the battle for the Aisne was still under way to the east. Far off a cow mooed again and again. 'Poor thing. Needs milking, I expect,' whispered Ruddock.

As they got to the deserted farm on the outskirts of the

village, they stopped and Gunn got them together. 'This is the most dangerous time,' he warned. 'We go through the village by bounds. And no shooting. Five minutes to rest and then we move. Quiet as mice now, boys; quiet as mice. We're nearly there.'

A pale, fitful moon was rising above the scudding clouds. Ruddock and Gunn acted as sentries as the soldiers sat down to rest. Guard and another disappeared to check the farmhouse, only to return a few minutes later with a large dog trailing at their heels.

'What the hell is that?' hissed Gunn.

'It's the dog that was locked up last night, sir,' explained Guard. 'It's in a bad way. We broke its chain and gave it some water and a biscuit. It's free now. We couldn't leave it to starve now, could we sir?'

Gunn received this in silence. Soldiers! He rolled his eyes. Sentimental idiots, sometimes. 'Fine. Well just make bloody sure that it doesn't start barking as we go through the village. Come on, let's go.'

They crept through the deserted village, moving almost on tiptoe from shadow to shadow. There wasn't a light anywhere and the deserted little streets seemed to magnify the echo of their boots. Slowly they worked their way down to the river bank, watching every dark patch for a sentry or an ambush – but nothing. Everything was dark and silent. Somewhere a cat yowled.

Finally they huddled on the damp riverbank grass in the shadow of the wrecked bridge. Gunn whistled across to the other bank. Nothing. He whistled again, louder. Still nothing.

A chill drizzle began to fall on the despondent little group.

'What now, sir?' said an anxious Ruddock.

'First thing is get your section stood to in all-round defence. Now I need to think,' replied Gunn. He eyed the home bank with a mixture of incredulity and irritation.

'Mebbe Sjt Doughty and the lads didn't get through?' said Ruddock with all the pessimism of the old soldier.

'Don't be silly. We'd have heard any firing,' snapped Gunn, but inwardly he wondered just what had happened.

'What do we do now sir?' said Lance Corporal Maddox, Ruddock's number two.

'We get across the river, that's what,' replied Gunn absently and with a confidence he didn't feel. He peered into the darkness of the far bank, hoping that his binoculars would help him see something - anything - and attract its attention. Nothing.

An uneasy quiet fall on the little group.

'Perhaps we could swim across?' said a voice, followed by, 'I can't bloody swim,' from another.

'Be quiet, the lot of you,' snapped Gunn. 'Anyone got a candle?'

They formed a close huddle, backs to the river, and Corporal Ruddock waved a shielded candle behind the wall of bodies. 'Someone on the far side is bound to see us,' Gunn said encouragingly. But no one did, and the candle kept blowing out.

He looked at his watch. Half past midnight. Five hours till dawn. Where the hell was C Company? Surely they hadn't abandoned them? How to get across the river? He wasn't a strong swimmer, but he didn't fancy ordering a soldier to do it in the dark.

An hour passed as the soldiers dozed while he scanned the far bank again and again. The water swirled by in the pale moonlight and he could swear that he could see what seemed to be the boats they had used two nights ago dragged up on the far shore. He wondered if they could find a place to hide during the day, one of the houses in the village, maybe…

He dozed.

Gunn woke with a start. A soldier was shaking his shoulder violently. 'Germans! Germans!' a voice hissed. 'On the bridge.'

Gunn was awake in a flash, heart pounding. The patrol was lying silent around him, listening, He saw a soldier's eyeballs gleam for a second as he mouthed in Gunn's ear, 'Huns, sir. On the bridge. Two of them. I can hear them, talking foreign.'

Heart in his mouth, Gunn edged under the half shattered bridge arch, treading on a Forester's leg in the process. He inched forward to hear the low murmur of voices; someone laughed. As the voices grew louder he suddenly realised that it wasn't English. He listened carefully and crept off to the side to see if he could see the Germans.

Then a voice laughed louder and he distinctly heard a voice say, '*Ah non, mon ami, ç'est impossible! Impossible.*'

French! Of course! They would be guarding the wrecked crossing point, just in case. He heaved a sigh of relief and called out quietly, '*Messieurs! Aidez moi.*'

The voices fell silent and he heard the click of a rifle being cocked.

'*Qui est là?*' shouted a voice.

'It's us. A British patrol', he added in English. He went on in French, 'We're stuck on the far bank. Twelve of us. We're under the bridge but we can't get back. Can you help?'

He heard the muttered conversation on the far side of the bridge. A French voice shouted, 'Show yourselves.' Cautiously the section emerged from under the bridge. 'Hold your rifles above your heads, boys,' said Gunn as they filed out into the last of the moon. He could see the silhouettes of two French soldiers looming on the far side of the broken bridge, rifles levelled down at the British group below.

'*Merde!*' exclaimed one. 'They are British.'

'Maybe it's a trick' said the other. 'Maybe they're spies.'

'We're not spies, you idiot!' half-shouted Gunn. He swore in French. 'I am Lieutenant Gunn of the Sherwood Foresters with a reconnaissance patrol with vital intelligence for GHQ and if you two imbeciles don't get your officer down here quickly I'll see you are doing sentry for the rest of this goddam war standing in a chamberpot full of shit.'

He paused for breath and reverted to English. 'Now move your fucking arses, because I can't stay here all night waiting to be captured by the Germans.'

There was a long silence. Then one of the sentries said to his colleague, 'I think they really are Rosbifs. *Vraiment!*'

An hour later the whole patrol was safely ashore. To Gunn's astonishment a large black dog jumped out of the second boat. Guard explained; 'It just kind of followed me, sir,' to hastily-suppressed grins.

As the boats were being stashed away by an amused pair of French infantrymen reeking of foreign tobacco and wine, Gunn insisted on seeing the two sentries who had saved them. He shook their hand in the growing dawn. 'How did you know we really were British?' he asked.

The more talkative of the two laughed and said, 'When you started shouting and cursing at us in French and then English, *M'sieur*. No *Boche* could do that.'

The French lieutenant who had brought them back across the river offered to accompany them back to the British HQ, but when they got to the big barn on the far side of Condé it was empty, although a pile of empty British ration tins in the corner confirmed that C Company had indeed been there. At the crest of the rise on the far side of the valley the Frenchman shook Gunn's hand and left them with the information that he thought that 'Captain Heddle' had taken his men back to Chassemy, about three kilometres south east. Wearily the little patrol fell in and started marching home.

What happened next is not entirely clear from the diaries, but piecing the fragmentary entries together it looks as if Gunn was not received well on his return to C Company. For example, the entry for 21st September reads:

Up before the CO. It seems that JH [Johnny Hedley, his company commander] *has put in a report that I disobeyed his orders by staying behind across the Aisne. His monkey was really up* [ie, he was in a bad temper] *when we got back and he told me that he could have me charged with desertion, which is absolute rubbish. When I pointed out that Sjt Doughty had brought back valuable intelligence and so had we, he pooh-poohed the whole thing and said that I should be sent home for recklessly endangering men's lives.*

I got a bit ratty and told him that <u>he had abandoned us</u> at the river and that if it wasn't for the French we'd all have ended up as prisoners thanks to him deserting us. He didn't like that and we had quite a row. Pity.

The CO was very good about it, though. He told me that Capt H. was right in strict theory but the intelligence that Cpl Ruddock and I had brought back had proved so valuable that it outweighed any other factors. He is a good man and v. fair. Even said that in my position he would probably have done the same. Sir Thomas is a jolly good CO and the chaps would follow him anywhere.

Anyway the upshot is that I am being moved from C Company. Don't know what's going to happen to me.

A bit fed up, though.

Gunn needn't have worried. Two days later he recorded in his diary:

22/3 September. Splendid news. GHQ has congratulated the battalion on the 'excellent and vital intelligence' we had provided, and the CO took me aside before lunch to tell me that our observations that the Germans were moving north had now been confirmed by the RFC. He said that he was pulling my platoon out of C Company and putting us with the m.g.s [machine guns] *as a sort of scouting and patrolling platoon in a kind of support role. As he pointed out, I am the senior subaltern and a brevet captain. I am delighted as are the men. JH is not so pleased, I am afraid. It's a shame as he is a good man but I get the feeling that he finds the responsibility makes him a bit windy.*

Tried to make it up with him at dinner last night but I fear he now bears me a grudge. Good as told me that I'd weakened his company by 11 platoon being moved to Bn HQ. True in a way, I suppose. Shame, as we should be fighting the Huns, not each other!

PS to diary: CO asked about my name today; coming from Nottingham, was it anything to do with Gunn and Moore? I explained that Billy Gunn, one of my uncles, had started the firm that makes the famous Gunn and Moore cricket bats. CO was pleased and asked why the lads call me Tommy; explained that Thaddeus not a great name but my initials 'T.O.M.' led to Tommy. I know that my parents named me after grandfather Thaddeus, but I think that's a bit Victorian nowadays!

* * *

Gunn's diary is important in that it records a major shift in the war and what was to lead to the extended trench lines of the Western Front. The Germans were now moving forces to the north to try and outflank the French and British just at the time that the BEF, balked on the Aisne, was moving north itself to be nearer its resupply lines and the Channel Ports. Thus was the 'race to the sea' born.

The diary also records a visit by the brigade commander, Brigadier General Drummond, who congratulated Gunn and his platoon on their exploits on the far bank of the Aisne. Gunn added that the adjutant later warned him that Captain Hedley was not impressed.

In the first week of October the battalion moved north – towards Belgium.

* * *

3 October

Today we set off marching south towards a place called Loupeigne. We march with the machine gunners now, well back in the column. The boys don't like it much. They prefer to be with their mates in the company. However we are followed by the MG's wagon, which carries their guns and a lot of ammunition. When the soldiers saw that they could pile some of their kit onto the m.g. wagon they soon changed their minds. The villages we pass through are deserted. Run down cottages, lots of dirt and only old men women and children standing at the doorways watching in silence as we go by. A bit different from the early days. One old boy spat in the road and called us cowards for marching the wrong way. Good job I was the only one who understood.

4 October

Rotten billets here. We all crammed into barns and cottages as best we could. Raining again. The locals offered us straw for the soldiers to lie on and then demanded money for it! Messing with Bn HQ officers now; a bit different from C Coy! Best behaviour! Bully beef, bread, cheese and wine for dinner. Tried to buy some food from the villagers but they say they have nothing except eggs. Surly lot. However, CO pretty relaxed and Maj. Carstairs has some good stories. Johnny Wybergh and I kipped in the kitchen last night. It's warm and it is getting nippy now the nights are drawing in. He tells me we are entraining tomorrow – for the north.

By 12 October the Foresters detrained at Béthune, just west of Lille, and started to march towards the sound of artillery to the east. As the battalion neared La Bassée they became victims of the increasingly desperate attempts by both sides to outflank each other as they moved north towards the Channel.

CHAPTER 5

INTO BATTLE –
LA BASSÉE, OCTOBER

When the Foresters detrained at Béthune none of them, from the Colonel to the youngest bugler, had the faintest idea what was going on.

A weary Rail Transport Officer had shrugged when Sir Thomas asked if there were any orders. Pressed by the Foresters' CO, the harassed RTO captain telephoned but could get no answer from his HQ. A frustrated Birkin then demanded who else had come through, to be told that the Norfolks had marched off to the east the evening before.

'Right!' said Birkin, 'Then we'll follow,' and the battalion fell in to face down the road towards La Bassée.

The Transport captain said despairingly, 'But what if orders come through, sir?' to which Birkin replied, 'Then tell 'em that I'm taking my battalion towards the sound of the guns! This La Bassée or whatever y'call it. And keep me informed, mind.

I'll leave two signallers as runners, man.' He pulled his horse's head to the east.

In a cold drizzle the battalion marched through deserted villages, while ahead the noise of the guns grew. As they trudged through Auchy les Mines, two shells thundered down in a field off to their right.

'Someone's spotted us,' muttered Johnny Wybergh.

Major Carstairs reined his horse in at the crossroads and pointed through the rain and mist. Far off, two slag heaps could be seen behind distant houses. 'That's where they'll be. An observation point. Up there. That's how they're directing their fire. It will be this crossroads. See for ruddy miles, from an OP up one of those things, I'll wager.'

As B Company trudged by, many of the soldiers stared off to the right, wondering what the second in command was pointing at. 'What's oop now?' said a voice. As if in reply, two more shells erupted well off to the left of the marching column, throwing huge black columns of smoke in the air. Carstairs and Wybergh eyed each other in alarm. 'Straddled, by God!' shouted Carstairs, 'Johnny, tell the companies to double, and quick. We don't want to get caught.'

In response to shouted orders the companies broke into double time and began to jog past the crossroads, to the accompaniment of much blaspheming by the soldiers. 'Never mind cursing, damn you,' bellowed Carstairs, wrenching his horse's head to make it stand still. 'Just keep moving. The next lot will probably land on your heads!'

He was right; two more shells crashed down, this time much closer. A man screamed and C Company in the rear broke ranks to spread out into the fields in artillery formation, doubling forward to get past the danger point. To Gunn and his platoon at the rear of the column it looked ominous. They were next to run the gauntlet.

The machine-gun serjeant looked doubtful and reined in his wagon. 'You're stopping?' called Gunn.

'Aye, sir. Happen we'll see where next two land, then we'll make a break for it. Ready lads?' he enquired of the marching files of the MG Section. Sure enough two more shells thundered down a few seconds later, one of them hitting the now empty crossroads itself, sending cobbles of *pavé* flying amid mushrooms of black smoke.

'Now, sir!' shouted the MG serjeant, and lashed his horses. They sprang forward and the wagon bounced behind. The soldiers alongside followed at a run.

'Come on boys,' echoed Gunn and his platoon, needing little encouragement. They sprinted past the crossroads, following the MG wagon. Two hundred yards into the fields beyond they stopped, chests heaving, to join the scattered members of C Company. Even as they were exchanging the usual lurid comments on the parentage of the German gunners, two more shells plunged in around the crossroads. A few dead Foresters lay motionless by the roadside.

'Fookin 'ell,' observed Private Bullock, succinctly summing up the soldiers' view of events.

Johnny Hedley was waiting, astride his horse. 'Ah, Gunn. Last as usual?' he enquired sarcastically.

Resentment boiled up in Gunn's breast, but then he felt a hand on his arm. Serjeant Doughty pointed down the road.

'Adjutant, sir,' he said as Johnny Wybergh clattered up. He had lost his hat and looked excited. He reined his mare in hard.

'C Company. Captain Hedley. Colonel's compliments and get your company into column of route and bring up the rear. Soon as you can, please. Gunn! The CO wants to see you as soon as possible. Quickly now.'

Gunn jogged to the head of the column, following the adjutant.

Lt Col Sir Thomas Birkin was puzzling over a map as he sat on his horse, while a captain of the Norfolks with an arm in a sling was looking up at him for his reaction. Gunn noticed that the sling was stained dark with dried blood. The Norfolk smiled at him. He looked very pale and tired and was splattered with mud.

The colonel looked up. 'Ah Gunn. Good man. I need you to find out what's happening over there.' He gestured to his left. 'Captain Thorne here tells me that the Norfolks' flank is in the air. Thinks there's some Frenchies somewhere out there but not sure. I want you to check if there's anyone on our left. No Germans. Can you ride?'

'Of course sir.'

'Good. Here's Major Carstairs' horse. Use that. Don't go too far. I just need to know what's happening on our left. I'll leave your platoon here to block the road, just in case. Want you back in one hour. Understood? One hour. No more.'

'Sir.' Gunn watched as Carstairs' horse was brought over. 'What about Major Carstairs, sir?'

Birkin looked at his adjutant. There was a pause. 'Dead, I'm afraid. Stopped to direct the battalion across the crossroads.

Hit by a piece of shell. Tragic.' His expression hardened. 'But that's war. Now be off with you, young Gunn. No heroics, mind; and I want you back here in one hour. I need to know. Now off you go.'

As Gunn swung into the saddle and turned to the north, Johnny Hedley and C Company marched by, heading for La Bassée. A voice from the ranks said audibly, 'Fook me, it's Mr Gunn on a 'orse. He moost 'ave bin promoted!' There was audible laughter.

'Quiet!' bellowed the Serjeant Major. Lt Col Sir Thomas Birkin grinned and slapped the rump of Carstairs' horse. 'One hour. No more,' he said as Gunn clattered down the road.

As Gunn trotted off to the north looking for whoever was there, the Foresters, led by the wounded Norfolks' major, marched down to a canal bank where they stopped and deployed. Colonel Birkin rode to the front and stared across the flat grey water at the mist. He scanned the distant villages and slag heaps for a long time.

'No sign of anyone out there,' he concluded. 'Where's your CO, Latimer?' he enquired of the Norfolks' major. 'I say, are you all right? You've gone very pale, old chap.'

The Norfolk waved vaguely out to his right. 'Down there, Colonel. Place called Douvrin. With the battalion.' His voice was slurred as he swayed and suddenly sat down on the ground. 'Told me to come and find you…' His voice tailed off and he fainted, falling sideways to lie unconscious.

'Stretcher bearers!' shouted Johnny Wybergh as he dismounted. He stopped and looked up as a red-tabbed Brigadier General, accompanied by a small posse of staff officers, came striding purposefully round the corner from the cottages by the roadside. He was a very tall, moustached figure with a shepherd's crook in his hand.

'Who the devil are you?' he shouted.

Birkin paused and saluted. 'Fourth Foresters, sir.'

'The blazes you are! Why are you late? And get off that damned horse. It's infantry action here, man.'

'Late sir? I have no orders…'

'Don't you dare argue with me, colonel. Get off that horse. You should have been here hours ago. Dammit, all I've got is the Norfolks and a promise of some blasted niggers from the Indian Corps, whenever they turn up. Now get your men deployed along the canal bank and watch out for the Huns. They're out there somewhere.' He gesticulated into the mist on the other side of the canal.

Birkin dismounted and moved closer to the Brigadier. Up close he could see that he wore Scots Guards buttons. 'General,' he began, 'I have my orders from GHQ…'

'Damn your impudence, sir!' shouted the Brigadier. 'Get your men deployed now.'

'My orders…'

'To the devil with your orders. Get your battalion deployed into line now or I'll have you relieved on the spot. D'you understand me, colonel?'

Birkin flinched. 'I hear your orders, General. But you should be aware that I have direct orders from Sir Archibald Murray to assemble here and wait for further orders.'

The tall brigadier paused. The name of the British Expeditionary Force's Chief of Staff carried some weight. 'So what brigade is your regiment?'

'None, General. We are the GHQ reserve battalion.'

The Guards brigadier tugged at his moustache. 'Hmmph. I see. Rear echelon men, what? Well, you've got your orders now. From me. You'll get a taste of front line soldiering now. Fall in on the left flank of the Norfolks. That'll be an assembly, won't it? And send runners to the Norfolks on your right and establish contact.'

'What about the left, General - to the north?'

'Don't know. It's Frenchies as far as we can make out. Cavalry. It's in the air.'

'And my orders from GHQ, general?'

'I don't give a damn about your orders, Colonel! Now is the moment, not some damned GHQ orders. If you're here, then you're assembled as far as I'm concerned. The Germans are going to attack on the other side of that ridge up there very soon and you are the only people who can stop them! Now get moving!'

As if on cue, half a dozen shells crashed down in the fields behind them. The Foresters dissolved into scattered individuals running along the line of the canal bank and dropping down into ditches and behind bushes. Within two minutes the regiment was nearly invisible; only the group of senior officers and the horses were left standing. Anther salvo crashed down, this time on the far bank of the canal.

'Time to go,' observed the Brigadier. 'You can find me at my HQ at the Marie at Douvrin. I will be keeping an eye on this battalion. Foresters, eh?' he added contemptuously. The group broke up, heading for the rear of the cottages, led by Birkin's groom. Birkin turned to go.

'Don't you salute, man?' demanded the Brigadier angrily.

'No. General. No we don't. Foresters do not salute in contact with the enemy. It's a lesson we learned the hard way. In South Africa.' He had noticed the lack of South African ribbons on the Guards officer's breast.

'And I'd get into cover if I were you, sir,' he added. 'Johnny!'

Birkin waved to his adjutant and the pair of them sprinted for the cover of a barn set back from the canal bank. Behind them, red faced with fury, the Guards brigadier stood alone as a burst of shrapnel shells erupted over the canal raising the water like a hailstorm.

'He's brave, damn him,' observed Birkin as they flopped onto a bale of hay. 'We'll set up battalion HQ here. Get the signallers and runners, Johnny.'

Johnny Wybergh looked out of the door at the tall figure striding away, imperiously waving his crook for his staff officers. 'He's a damn fool, if you ask me, Colonel. Thank God I'm not a Guardsman.'

Birkin smiled. 'Me too, Johnny; me too.'

Even as they spoke a hail of bullets and shells fell all around, and through the mist long lines of grey-clad soldiers came into view on the ridge to the east. There was no time for fire orders – every soldier with a rifle opened fire at the targets across the canal, which wavered and then, shredded by the intense fire, went to ground. Off to the right the stuttering of one of the Foresters' machine guns added to the havoc among the German formations.

Three miles to the north Tommy Gunn heard the sudden

outbreak of firing. It coincided with his own collision with a French roadblock outside a village called Ligny le Petit, where a nervous French cavalryman fired at the strange figure looming out of the mist from the south. Fortunately for Gunn the badly-aimed shot from the notoriously-inaccurate French carbine missed, prompting a thoroughly-alarmed Gunn to unloose a volley of fluent French curses on the frightened sentry.

It turned out that the man was part of the cavalry screen between La Bassée and Armentières, twenty miles to the north. An elegant cavalry officer appeared, smoking a cheroot and confirmed that he was part of Maud'huy's Tenth Army and that the Germans were massing to the east around Lille. In return Gunn explained that the BEF was now in La Bassée.

'You British will advance? Attack?' asked the cavalry captain, stroking his moustache.

Gunn replied with a very Gallic shrug. 'Who can tell, my friend? I am just a lieutenant of infantry.'

'Better you do,' responded the Frenchman. 'The Boche must be ejected from the soil of France. It is our sacred duty.'

Gunn wrote the Foresters' details in his field notebook and exchanged the page with the Frenchman's location and regiment; the Second Dragoons. Then with a handshake, the gift of a cheroot and a salute, he clattered off back to the south and La Bassée.

By the time he got back to his platoon, deployed across the road facing north, it was obvious that a serious battle was in progress somewhere behind them. Shrapnel burst over the line of the canal and bullets were cracking everywhere. Serjeant

Doughty stared back at the woolly bears and mushrooms of black smoke from the Jack Johnsons lining the canal.

'Someone's coppin' it sir,' he observed dispassionately.

'Where's battalion HQ?'

'Down this road, sir. Brown wooden barn at the crossroads. At least according to Captain Hedley.'

Gunn felt a twinge of alarm. 'Captain Hedley?'

'Aye, sir. When we were told to come here, Captain Wybergh told us to take orders from C Company until further notice.' He pointed to an isolated whitewashed cottage with a red tiled roof about three hundred yards away, near the canal bank. 'That's company HQ sir.'

Gunn picked up the reins. 'Damn silly place. It's an obvious target. He'd be far better off in an open field.' He shook his head. 'Well, if anyone asks, I am back and reporting direct to the Commanding Officer as ordered. Understood?'

'Very good sir.'

As Gunn cantered off to the south, Doughty watched him with a faint smile. He liked Gunn.

At battalion HQ Gunn received a warm reception, centred mainly on a scalding hot tin mug of Serjeant Major's tea, well laced with rum. Colonel Birkin listened in silence as he related his story, taking the piece of paper and checking the French cavalry's details on the map. He scribbled a note and passed it to a runner.

'Get yourself to Brigade HQ at the mayor's office in the middle of Douvrin and give them this," he said. "Get a reply.' The signaller scuttled away.

Birkin swilled his tea. 'And you, young Gunn, well done.

Now you'd better get back to your platoon. Probably a good thing to stay on that road looking north. Left flank roadblock, that kind of thing.' He stood up, as did Gunn.

'Sorry about Major Carstairs, sir.'

Birkin nodded. 'Bad show. Hit by a whole chunk of *pavé*. Smashed in his skull. Not pretty - but quick. He was a good soldier. We'll miss him. I'll write to his widow later.' He sighed. 'Three officers dead already. Bad show. Now off you go. Report to Captain Hedley.'

What happened next is best taken from Gunn's diary, written after the events at La Bassée.

> *17th October 1914*
>
> *This has been a very bad few days. The bn detrained at Béthune, then marched to a place called La Bassée. We were shelled at a crossroads and poor old Major Carstairs was killed. I was sent off on his horse to find out what was on our left. Fr. cavalry from 10th Army (I think).*
>
> *When I got back I found that the pl. had been put back under C Company. Johnny Hedley was a bit difficult. Told him that the CO had said we should stay as a roadblock facing north but he ordered us to move and go forward about two hundred yards front left. Even said 'you're taking orders from me now, Gunn' in front of the soldiers.*
>
> *Got to a grassy bank with a hedge and took cover. There was a cobbled sunken lane down in front of us. Could see quite a long way. There was a little wood off to our left and I wanted to send a patrol out to see if it was*

clear but JH told me pretty sharply to stay where we were and not to go forward. (Actually said, 'no more fancy stunts from you, Gunn!')

After about an hour a tall brigadier general came up with his staff captain, a captain in the Norfolks. The general was using a shepherd's crook. He said he was checking the brigade's left flank. Something about it being in the air.

He was quite cross and asked me why we hadn't moved forward. I told him that this was where we had been ordered to stay. He said that he would cross the lane and get to a better vantage point. I started to warn him about the little wood to our left but he started shouting at me and asking why if I was concerned I hadn't shown some initiative and gone and scouted it, so I told him about JH's orders. He went down the bank onto the lane with the Staff Captain and then an mg opened up from the wood. Bullets just pouring down the lane. I could even see sparks where they hit the cobble stones.

It was horrible. The general was twisted and flung down and the captain's head seemed to blow apart. They were only about ten yards in front of us but we were in cover behind the bank. The general lay kicking like a rabbit for a few seconds than stopped. I could only see the captain's legs but he was still.

I was about to jump down and see if I could help the general when Cpl Ruddock stopped me and said there'd only be another dead officer. He threw a haversack into the lane and that got another burst of fire right in front of our noses. I decided to wait for dark (it was just getting dusk) when *after about ten minutes J. Hedley appeared demanding to know who was firing at what. I explained about the general and he peered through the hedge then rounded on me shouting, 'and you left them there?' He called us cowards and said that he would see if the general was all right and that he might just be wounded and we could have killed him by not trying rescue him.*

He started to push through the hedge. We tried to tell him about the Hun mg, but he just brushed us aside and jumped down into the lane. He started to turn and said something like, 'You see? There is no machine gun,' when he was cut down by a single burst. I was so close I saw the bullet hit his chest. He went down.

I sent Ruddock and his section to go out to the left and stalk the little wood. Just as it got dark we heard some shooting and shouting and Ruddock's men came back later with a big brass Maxim he had captured. He told me that there had been a German mg team of four and that they had taken them by surprise. Kearey had bayonetted a German and showed me a Pickelhaube helmet he'd taken as a souvenir.

Ruddock had collected all the dead Germans' papers and their shoulder flashes. Good man. Told Ruddock to report to Bn HQ and brief the adjutant.

We got the BG's body in after dark. He and the Norfolk captain were both dead with several wounds. JH was still alive but unconscious and the stretcher bearers took him away. It looks like he's taken just one bullet on the right side of his chest. No exit wound so must still be in there.

As he was being taken away someone in the platoon muttered 'he wor a bloody fool.' I told him pretty sharply to shut up. Couldn't see who in the dark.

A horrible business. The upshot is that I am now OC C Coy until further notice. The Huns made several attacks mainly against B coy to our right and the Norfolks, but we drove them off. We lost 8 men, including Sjt Maxwell of 12 pl. Johnny Townsend hit and gone back to base but walking wounded only, according to the signallers – who get to hear everything first, naturally.

Got relieved two days later by some Indians from the Lahore Corps. Did not impress. Cold and miserable lot. Low morale. I wouldn't rely on them.

The bn. is now in billets back near Béthune trying to reorganise and clean up. Amazing what sleep, decent food and the rum ration will do! The rascals have even started playing footie again in the square!

Johnny Wybergh told me that the Norfolks had lost over 200 men and a dozen officers, including the major who had been our guide. He'd lost too much blood. We've had over 60 casualties including 5 officers. Amazing. Apparently B coy were shelled quite heavily and lost over 30 men including poor old Makepeace, who has disappeared completely with the whole of B Coy HQ. Berry has the company now.

Johnny also told me that the bn. should never have been diverted at La Bassée and there had been the deuce of a row over BG Fitzjohn 'stealing' the Foresters, because we were meant to be heading north to a place called Ypres, but as he was dead now there would be no official report and complaint.

I never want to live through this again. We had no spades to dig and had to use our mess tins to dig trenches and funkholes. What made it worse was that we had no food and no water for two days. We took food and ammo from the dead. And it was so cold and wet.

The shells are the worst. I saw young Cpl Simpson's body after he was killed. It was like chunks of meat. Sickening. We just shovelled it into a blanket and buried him in a makeshift grave in the garden of an abandoned cottage. I could hardly bear to watch. I noticed that the boys dug up all the potatoes and carrots too!

Somehow I can't see this war being over by Christmas. And I can't see us keeping going with all these casualties.

***

Gunn was right about that, but not about the casualties. Next day the Foresters moved north - to Ypres.

CHAPTER 6

YPRES; MESSINES, 21 OCTOBER – 1 NOVEMBER

The Foresters received a draft of 50 men and three officers at Béthune and were then moved by train to Hazebrouck on the Belgian border. Both sides were now feeling for the other's flanks as they moved north in what became known as 'the Race to the Sea.' There were a number of collisions and encounter battles in north-east France during October 1914: at Armentieres, La Bassée (where the Foresters were involved) and ultimately in Belgium at Ypres itself.

At the time no one thought of the Ypres area as the grim static trench war that it was to become for the next three and a half years. The BEF thought they were advancing, as Gunn's diary makes plain.

21 October 2014

Detrained at a place called Hazebrouck near the Belgian border and marched east to Balleuil (I think I have that right.) The coy is in barns on the Ypres (funny spelling) road with A to the east facing a place called Messines and B to the south east covering the Armentières road. D as usual in reserve in the middle of the town. Lucky beggars!

CO came round at last light to see we were all right. Fortunately I had posted sentries on the roads and ordered 10 pl. out as a picquet at dusk, so he was jolly complimentary. I told him that that was what I had learned to do in India. He had brought up a couple of bottles of champagne for the coy officers and walked round all the soldiers in the barns. Had a good word for everybody.

Afterwards he sat in coy HQ (a big farmhouse with the farmer's family still in residence) and talked to us round the kitchen stove for a while. The farmer was most impressed by 'milord Birkin!' and opened a bottle of cognac which the CO insisted on sharing with us and the farmer, much to M'sieur Jaan's delight. He is Flemish, like all the locals round here, but (thank goodness) speaks good French. CSM Rogers came in with some reports and the CO insisted he join us in a glass, much to the Sjt Maj's surprise!

There is some fighting going on to the east and we can hear the guns and at night see the flashes as the sky is lit up. The CO says the Corps' plan is to advance east to a place called Menin and outflank the Germans but the Germans are attacking back so it's stopped any advance. (He called it an 'encounter battle.')

Without a map it is difficult to work out what is going on, but the CO tells us we are to remain in reserve at one hour's notice to move. The CSM muttered, 'Suits me sir, after La Bassée!' and Birkin laughed.

He is the best kind of colonel. We are lucky. As he was leaving he took me to one side and said quietly to me that the 2ⁿᵈ Battalion had been in action at La Vallée, where they had been cut off and surrounded and reduced to 2 officers and 60 men before they were overwhelmed by the Germans. Apparently poor old Hobbs had been killed along with several others. Dreadful news. And to think I had asked for a posting to the Second, back in August!

Gunn's diary only tells half the story. By 25 October it was plain that the Ypres battle had turned into a ferocious slugging match. The Foresters as GHQ reserve were warned for action several times but stood down as the situation stabilised and the line held. On 29th October they moved forward to Kemmel and found rough and ready billets as they waited for orders.

Nevertheless the situation was becoming graver by the day as casualties mounted and battalions were shredded away by unheard-of casualties. Gunn records getting a draft of 30 men and one lieutenant to C Company on 27 October but noted that the company was still 20% below strength.

On 30 October the Foresters were finally warned at short notice to advance east to shore up the Messines ridge, where massed German formations looked like breaking through after a series of heavy bombardments and frontal attacks. This time the battalion was thrown into the furnace of the final battles known as 'First Ypres.'

"Right gentlemen! Saddle up and let us get started. Marching order, heavy packs and greatcoats on the wagons with the company quartermaster.'

Acting Captain Gunn surveyed his platoon commanders and the CSM as they huddled in the doorway of the Jaans' kitchen: Meynell, Miller and Thruxton, the new second lieutenant from the draft. They looked cheerful enough, he decided. The prospect of action, of movement, raised their spirits. Anything was better than the inaction of the previous week, with its stories of heavy fighting and heavy losses.

Gunn wasn't so sure. After La Bassée he had doubts about the whole thing. Modern war wasn't like India or even South Africa, he realised. He looked at young Lt Meynell, fresh-faced and up from the Depot with his earlier draft. He was busy scribbling in his notebook and Gunn felt a pang of some indescribable emotion, wondering just how many of them would survive what he expected to be a fairly bloody affair.

Instead he said, 'Right gentlemen, you have your orders. Keep your platoons tight under your control. The Sarn't Major will be at company HQ with me and the Colour Sarn't will make sure that you get ammunition, food and water. But keep your men well in hand and keep their heads down. No stupid heroics. Any questions?'

There were none, and the orders group dispersed to their posts. Within the hour they were on the march, heading east towards the ridge between Wyschaert ("Whitesheet") and Messines. By last light on the 30th they were huddled in a hamlet called Sauvegarde by a crossroads. On the Messines Ridge to their front they could see the German shells bursting as they tried to force the cavalry brigade deployed as infantry back off the crest.

The next morning there was a bombardment along the ridge just west of Messines. Gunn thought he'd never seen shellfire like it as the ridge erupted in shell bursts and then the German infantry attacked. They could hear the incessant rattle of rifles and machine guns. All day the Foresters watched the fighting on the ridge as the Germans closed in and were flung back. Occasionally a random shell came over and landed on the fields near the Foresters.

Gunn and the serjeant major huddled in a barn door cold, soaked and miserable, watching the rain come down. Eventually the CO and RSM appeared and after a few pleasantries went to talk to the knots of soldiers trying to stay dry.

'No orders yet, young Gunn,' said the colonel. 'I hear that a reserve battalion is being brought up at last light to shore up the cavalry. He jerked his chin towards the smoke-shrouded ridge. 'I think they're taking a hell of a beating up there.'

CSM Rogers shook his head. 'Rather them than us, sir.'

'You're right, serjeant major,' Birkin said, 'but if we're ordered in that's where we'll be, I suspect.'

A shell rumbled overhead like an express train and crashed into a field about two hundred yards behind them. Everyone ducked instinctively at the eruption of black smoke. Birkin watched the smoke drifting away.

'Five nines, gentlemen. Heavy stuff. And the Hun's not short of ammunition either. Not like us. We are down to a couple of days' shells, the RA major tells me. So if we're sent in, then it's down to accurate musketry once again.'

He stared at the ridge. 'Anyway, if we do have to go forward I've told Teddy Tulloch to put one of his machine guns with you. He can fire down the front of the line as C Company will be left flank. I've told him to join you and move as much ammunition as you can carry. We might need it. Understood?' With a wave of his walking stick, the CO headed back to battalion HQ.

The day wore on and the fighting on the ridge died down. At dusk a procession of brightly-painted London buses drove through Sauvegarde, with Scots soldiers on board, much to the amusement of the Foresters. The buses stopped on the outskirts of the village and soldiers began to debus.

'Funny looking Jocks,' said CSM Rodgers. 'They've got pink kilts. Or am I seeing things?'

Gunn agreed and watched as a lanky figure walked back to the village. It turned out to be a lieutenant indeed wearing a greyish pink kilt, who introduced himself in impeccable Mayfair tones as 'Mr Cameron-Taylor, D Company, London Scottish.'

'Blimey,' said CSM Rogers quietly. 'Territorials. Weekend warriors. They must be getting bloomin' desperate.'

Gunn shushed him and shook the stranger's hand. 'Gunn. Commanding C Company, Four Foresters. What's going on?'

'My CO told me to warn you that we're going to deploy here and then go up the ridge. He's spoken to your colonel. Just wanted to make sure that you knew what's going on. It'll be dark soon.'

Gunn nodded. 'Sensible. We might have potted at you. What's the plan? Dig in and reinforce the cavalry? They've taken a pounding up there.'

'Oh no,' said the Scot. 'We're deploying for a night attack, forward of the ridge.'

Gunn was flabbergasted. He stared at the ridge a mile away, fuming like a range of volcanoes. 'Attack? Not dig in? You mean go forward?'

Cameron-Taylor smiled. 'That's the idea. Fixed bayonets in the dark. That should winkle the Hun out, what?'

Gunn was not so sure. He had a pretty good idea that a lot of Germans were just over the ridge and that the best thing the London Scottish could do was get onto it and dig in in defence; but it wasn't his business and he shut up.

'I'll send a runner back if need be,' said the Scotsman. 'Stay in touch. That sort of thing.' He shook hands. 'Goodbye.'

Dunn watched him go. 'Good luck,' he shouted after him.

The Scot replied with a cheery wave. 'Thanks, old boy. See you later.'

'If you ask me,' said CSM Rogers, 'I think that lot are going to cop it. Straight up, sir.'

Gunn was going to tell Rogers that no one had asked him, but thought better of it. Rogers was a steady old regular, efficient, well-respected by the soldiers and not worth upsetting. He might need him. Instead he said, 'How long've you been in, Sarn't Major?'

'Seventeen years, sir. Joined as a boy bugler at Derby. Walked from me dad's farm at Clay Cross to enlist.' He looked out at the gathering dusk. 'I can still blow a bugle better than soom of the useless articles the band and drums have today.'

Gunn smiled. 'Where have you served?'

'Ireland, India, South Africa. The Depot. Bin in both regular battalions. Second was stricter back then. Bit heavy, if you take my meaning. First battalion always had a lighter feel, if you know what I mean.' He took off his cap and scratched his head. 'And now this. Tell you the truth, sir, I never imagined it would end oop like this. Never.' As if on cue, a line of red flashes suddenly lit up the darkening ridge and the rumble of artillery thundered across the fields. 'Soom poor bugger's coppin' it.'

'Well at least it's stopped raining,' said Gunn. 'What's the ration situation?'

The serjeant major grinned. 'Q Smith has scrounged a whole box of bully and he's making an all-in stew back at the old barn behind that first farm. Potatoes and everything in dixies. Got the wagon up after we got here and told me he's got a jar of rum for the morning as well.'

Gunn was impressed. He'd been expecting a tin of cold bully.

'Oh, don't you worry sir. Smith'll see that the lads are looked after, never fear.'

'And he'll check the rum for quality, I expect?' Gunn laughed.

Rogers joined in. 'Well tha'll not be wanting lads to get bad rum, now would thee, sir?' He walked out into the gloom. 'I'll just get round the lads, sir. See they're alreet. You'll be putting sentries out?'

Gunn gave a guilty start. Back here behind the front line he'd forgotten to post sentries, and he wondered if that was the serjeant major's way of jogging his memory.

'Thank you S'arnt Major,' he said. 'I'll walk out with the platoon commanders and post them myself.'

'Good idea, sir. And I'll make sure that Belfield has your meal ready when you get back.' With that Rogers nodded amiably, saluted, tugged his moustache, straightened his shoulders and disappeared in the darkness. A minute later Gunn heard him telling some luckless Forester to sort himself out amid a volley of colourful language. He was lucky, he decided, to have such a solid serjeant major.

By the time Gunn had got back, it was after eight o'clock. It was cold and dark and a chill wind made things colder, although it helped to dry out his uniform. Overhead the stars glinted through the scudding clouds. Belfield was sheltering in the corner of the little barn with the CSM. Both were scraping contentedly at mess tins as Richards, the company signaller, mopped up the last of his meal with a hunk of bread. A strong aroma of beef stew hung in the air. Belfield pushed a hot mess tin, heavy with bully and potatoes, into Gunn's hand and the serjeant major passed over a mug of hot tea.

'Thank you. By God, I'm starving. How are the boys?'

'They're all right, sir. They're drying out in the barn. Plenty of good snap inside them, thanks to the Q bloke, and I've told them there's rum for the morning. There's some bread for thee 'ere. Sentries?'

Gunn paused between welcome mouthfuls. 'Two up the Whitesheet road, two up the Messines road. Told the platoon commanders it's two hours on, with the first man changing after one hour so that there's always one new man on every hour. Platoon commanders to inspect. I'll take a walk round around two o'clock.'

Rogers nodded appreciatively. 'Good. If you like I'll walk round about midnight. That lets you get your head down for a bit, sir. Wake you at one ack emma?'

'Sounds about right, sarn't major. When you see Q Smith you can congratulate him on his stew. Excellent.'

Gunn finished his stew, went outside, relieved himself and settled down on a pile of straw in a dark corner of the barn, to fall asleep immediately.

It seemed he'd hardly closed his eyes when the serjeant major was shaking him.

'Best coom, sir. Summat's up.' Gunn followed him outside to join a huddle of Foresters in the moonlight staring into the darkness at the ridge. It looked as if it was on fire. 'What's the time?'

'Just gone nine. That's those London Scots. Christ knows what they're doing, but someone's taking a beating.' The rattle of rifle fire drifted on the breeze. Gunn and the Foresters stayed watching as the ridge burned and flickered on the skyline.

'Any orders, S'arn't major?'

'Nowt, sir. You want me to send a runner to battalion HQ?'

'No. Leave it.' Gunn thought for a second. 'No. Just double the sentries and we'll take it from there.' He was dog tired. 'Wake me at one and I'll do the rest of the night. And keep an eye on that ridge.'

'Very good sir.'

Gunn was woken at one o'clock by Belfield and a mug of scalding tea. Frowsty with sleep, he stumbled out into a clear cold night. CSM Rogers was standing in the moonlight watching Messines Ridge. It had quietened down, but there was still a fire burning somewhere on the far side and occasional rifle fire drifted on the breeze.

'Morning, sarn't major.' He yawned. The scalding tea burned his lips and he rubbed his stubbly chin.

'Morning sir. It's gone quiet the last hour. Private Guard says it's a mill burning up there.' He glanced at his company commander. 'He went forward with Kearey. Foraging, they say.' Rogers kept an impassive face, staring up at the ridge.

Gunn stole a glance at the serjeant major. The light from the barn illuminated his features. Gunn wasn't sure if he was suppressing a laugh. 'Guard left the company? Foraging?'

'That's what they said, "Foraging, sir."' He nodded at the ridge. 'Kearey said he'd spotted the abandoned farm halfway up there. Gone up to check it was clear, so he says. Caught the pair of them sneaking back with a sack'

'Looting?' To the army of 1914, looting was a serious offence.

Rogers pulled a face. 'Not really. Not looting as such. More… *scrounging* as they call it.'

'Scrounging? Such as?'

'Well, he can tell you 'isself. Guard! Over here.'

Private Guard emerged from the dark, clutching a large and obviously heavy potato sack. He stood rigidly to attention, staring blankly over Gunn's shoulder.

'What's in that sack?'

'Grub. For the company, sir.'

'Tip it out, man.'

Guard did so and half a dozen very dead hens, four ducks and a pile of potatoes and carrots tumbled out. Last, a bottle red wine rolled out, to land with a soft thump on the earth. He looked at Gunn.

'Farm's empty sir. It would only go to waste.'

Gunn scratched his bristly chin. 'So you helped yourself. Anyone in the farm?'

'No sir. Deserted. Left in a hurry. Not a soul. Honest, sir.'

'Hmmm. You know that looting is a very serious crime?'

'Sir. But I only wanted to see that it didn't go to waste. Seemed a shame just to leave them all there, sir. Not fed. On their own, like. Not right. I mean, the Germans could get it, couldn't they?'

Gunn looked at Rogers and tried hard to keep a straight face. 'Well this is a damn serious business, Private Guard. Stealing from our allies.' He paused. 'But they did abandon it and we must ensure that things like this don't fall into German hands. And we are at war and we have to live as best we can.'

He came to a decision. 'Right. Give all this to Q Smith. Maybe he'll be able to do something with it. And don't get caught doing this again.'

'Sir. Thank you, sir. And the wine?'

'Yes. Give that to the Q bloke too. Maybe the company cooks can make *coq au vin* with it. Dismiss.'

A relieved Guard gathered up his loot and fled into the darkness. Rogers smothered a laugh. 'Good one sir, if I may say so. You'll never stop them scrounging. Never. That's soldiers.'

'At least it was food. If it had been silver or

valuables I'd have had to crime him. Where's Kearey by the way?

'On stag, sir. Out on the Messines road. He was the one who put them up to it, I'm sure.'

'Hmm. Well, see he gets the message too.'

Gunn spent the rest of the night walking round the sleepy sentries in the moonlight and keeping a watchful eye on the ridge. The fire died down by dawn and he stood the company to as the sky lightened to the east. As the light strengthened he could see scattered distant figures trailing back down the slope. Through his binoculars he could see they were British.

'Ours?' said a voice at his elbow. It was Teddy Tulloch, the machine gun officer, warmly wrapped in his greatcoat. 'Damned cold this morning.'

'Hello, Teddy. Yes. Ours. Looks like those London Scottish we saw yesterday. Looks like they're falling back.'

Tulloch stared at the ridge. 'Well, according to the CO we're about to go up there any time soon. Plug the gap or something. I left him and Johnny scribbling orders'

Tulloch was right. Half an hour later the Foresters were ordered onto the Messines Ridge with orders to dig in on the left of the cavalry troopers in Messines. Gunn's diary takes up the story:

We went up to Messines ridge in artillery formation about an hour after dawn. It was bitterly cold. Thank God the men had had their tea and rum. No breakfast. We had to lug big heavy boxes of ammo for the mgs up there as well, one box between two men, which made for a slow advance. Passed some of the London Scottish dribbling back (in disarray, to be honest.) I spoke to a few of them and they looked shocked. Quite a lot of walking wounded.

Purely by chance I bumped into their CO, a Lt Col Monroe (I think), coming down the ridge. He told me that they had been attacked the previous night just as the Scots were trying get organised on the ridge to advance. Told me they hadn't been expecting the Huns to try a night attack.

Apparently the Germans were driven back by rifle fire and a series of bayonet charges. He told me that it was a completely confused struggle in the dark. They could see the Huns by the light of a burning mill and some haystacks, and there was hard fighting, with bayonets and fire exchanged at close quarters. He told me that officers, sergeants and men just had to act on their own initiative in the dark as they ran into the Germans.

Reading between the lines it sounds a complete shambles and later, as we dug in, we heard from one of the cavalrymen that the London Scottish had been forced back off the ridge in the dark with terrible casualties . I asked a wounded Scot that Thompson and Henries brought in if he knew of a Mr Cameron-Taylor. He told me that the officer had led a bayonet charge in the dark but didn't know what had happened to him.

Apparently one of the big problems was their Territorial Forces rifles. They had been issued with the Mark I pattern Enfield Ross, converted to take Mark VII ammunition ; but the front stop clips were the wrong shape for our BEF rounds. Consequently, the rifles could only be used as single-loader. Unbelievable! One of the soldiers told me that every time he fired his rifle, his bayonet fell off. Hardly conducive to modern warfare!

1 November
Got dug in on the Messines Ridge. We could see for miles. Fantastic field of fire. There's a burned out mill to our left and lots of dead bodies lying around, both British and German. There are two locked together about a hundred yards in front. Through the glasses I could see that it was one of the Scots and a German who seem to have bayonetted each other. Awful. Very tired but must see that the platoons are properly dug in. Don't want what happened the London Scots to happen to us.

The Germans did attack the Messines Ridge again over the next two days but were driven back by the Foresters, thanks mainly to the machine gun section. The battalion war diary records that "the two Maxim Vickers fired over 12,500 rounds mainly in enfilade across the front of the battalion thereby breaking up numerous German infantry attacks."

On 2 November the Foresters were relieved by the Kings Own Yorkshire Light Infantry and pulled back into reserve . Gunn records:

Relieved by 2 KOYLI who were grumbling that they'd only just come out of the line and had been turfed out of reserve in a rest camp (they said) near Estaires to the rear to come and relieve us. They looked a tough bunch. Mainly little men. Miners I think. One of their officers told me that they were down to 350 men and 15 officers – and they were one of the more up to strength battalions! That can't be true.

Tulloch's machine guns saved the day for us on the ridge, I am sure. They tore into the lines of Germans, who were extraordinarily brave but very foolish to advance in such massed formations. At one point Sjt Lacey's gun (the one with us) started to jam. Everything very muddy and no gun oil. Things looked dicey but Teddy Tulloch appeared running through a perfect storm of bullets and gave Lacey a big tin of ration margarine which they upended on top of the gun. As the gun was hot it melted and ran all over the action! Instant gun oil! Very ingenious. The gun fired well after that but the smell of cooking caused a few comments.

Am damn' glad to be out of it. Messines Ridge was hellish; exposed and dangerous. The weather was cold, wet and beastly. No real trenches and lots of German sniping, interspersed with occasional crumps of artillery. Pretty accurate too.

I talked to an Irish trooper of the 5th Dragoon Guards who had managed to dig a sort of one-man trench behind a bush, and he said that he was the only survivor of his section of 8! Rest all killed or wounded. He made me laugh when he said "I didn't enlist in the cavalry for this, Sorr!" He'd been there a week he thought and told us that what was left of the 4th cavalry brigade was fighting in Messines village about a mile to our right. There was certainly something going on there. We could hear firing all day.

That night I sent a section from every pl. forward to lie out as picquets about a hundred yards forward of our line in case the Huns tried another stunt at night. They didn't; but when the posts returned at dawn they brought in over 300 German identity discs and lots of papers from searching the dead. Good work; but I noticed that a lot of the soldiers seemed suddenly to be sporting wrist watches!

The company lost another 6 killed and 10 wounded during these last two days, as well as young Peter Thruxton who was killed by a shell splinter that almost cut him in half. Poor boy. He's only been in France a week. The CO says he will write to the family.

Late entry. Richards the signaller tells me that Johnny Townsend has rejoined A Company. It was a shrapnel ball that sliced his scalp apparently. We get a lot of head wounds from these 'woolly bears' and their confounded shrapnel.

<u>*Even later entry*</u>*. (after midnight on 2/3 November) When we arrived at these billets back in Wulvergem, met by CQMS Smith. Very. cheerful. He had prepared some kind of poultry stew for the company, of all things! A bit thin but hot and plenty of biscuit. The boys are exhausted so this cheered them up, as did lashings of hot tea and roaring fires. Q insisted on giving me a separate mess tin. Told me it was specially prepared for me, "thanks to Private Guard's scrounging the other night." That seems like another age now.*

It turned out to be the company cooks' idea of Coq au Vin! Not exactly the Ritz's version but still chicken stew in red wine. Shared it with the CSM, who is equally tired and told me that he'd had a couple of close shaves up on the ridge. We're all very tired. Company roll call: only 72 men and 3 officers. This can't go on.

Gunn was wrong. The BEF's ordeal at Ypres was just getting under way.

CHAPTER 7

CRISIS AT YPRES - NOVEMBER

Having failed on the 31st October to break through on the Menin Road (when a bayonet charge by 2 Worcesters had driven the victorious Germans back at Gheluvelt) and at Messines Ridge, the German High Command opted for one last big offensive around Ypres to drive the BEF and the French into the sea.

The plan was to push a powerful force of the Kaiser's élite Prussian Guard Corps down the Menin road, plus concentric attacks all round Ypres, all supported by the fire of 238 heavy guns. There were 16 fresh German infantry and 6 cavalry divisions in ten corps, massed against the salient with at best seven understrength and exhausted BEF divisions with 3 weak cavalry divisions and 5 Indian brigades.

Gunn's diary takes up the tale.

5 November 1914

A few quiet days. Wonderful to get washed, put on clean kit and get some sleep. Checked all the rifles first morning. All immaculate, and without any chivverying from the offrs or NCOs. You could have taken them to the Bisley Rifle meeting! Very few kit losses. I am so proud of the soldiers. They grumble and get into scrapes but they are as brave as lions and will stick anything. No wonder they call the Foresters the 'Nails'.

Post came up about mid-morning (letters from mother and father with a parcel from home plus another card from Dorothy) and the CO came round at lunch time and messed with the officers – all 3 of us. We ate cold chicken sandwiches and drank whisky out of mugs with water that tasted of chloride of lime. I provided mother's cake from the parcel. Jolly good too. CO in good spirits. He told us that the Bn was down to 420 men and 21 officers, but new drafts expected soon. After lunch he walked round the men and talked to a lot of them before heading off to B Company who have had a much worse time. Charles Berry has only one officer.

6 November

Warned for a brigadier's inspection tomorrow. Bit of a panic and much kit cleaning. Cadged a horse from the transport lines and rode into Kemmel this afternoon. Managed to buy two local tourist maps, lots of metal polish for the coy and some wine as well as have an omelette in a cafe. Forgotten what clean folk looked like!

Back at coy HQ saw the CSM and I would inspect the coy at 0900 tomorrow to make sure we are tickety boo for 11.00 and gave him the brass polish and a bottle of wine. Spent the evening going over the map of the Ypres region with the two pl. comds making sure we knew where all the key points were. They've drawn little maps in their FS ¹Note Books. They're good men.

7 November

Slept well and undisturbed. Bright, dry day, thank goodness. Up, washed and shaved. Belfield has got my kit looking half decent and then inspected the coy. Who would have believed it! Couple of days ago they looked like bearded ruffians from some pantomime about pirates - now they are immaculately turned out, uniforms clean, puttees straight, with rifles and brasses gleaming. Looked as if they were mounting guard at the Palace. Only thing is that lots of caps have gone missing. Can't be helped.

Marched the coy to Nieuwkirke where the battalion is parading and fell in. Lots of men and even some officers without caps. Looks strange. Saw J. Townsend. Looks as if he's wearing a white turban! B Coy dreadfully thin on parade. Inspection was by a Brig Gen G J Cuthbert commanding 13 Bde. He did it on foot and spoke to a lot of the men.

When he got to us he was very decent, asked me what sort of time we'd had and would I point out any soldiers who had done well. Of course they've all done pretty well. He stopped at Kearey (whose scar was bound to invite comment) and asked him what had happened to his face. 'Sure, did it not get ripped open by a bullet down by that river, Sorr,' says Kearey, bold as brass. I explained that it was on the Marne and Kearey had never left the ranks, apart from getting stitched up by the doc at the time. 'Remarkable,' says the BG. 'Looks a nasty wound.' Then turns to me and says 'have you put him in for an award?' I stammered out some rot about not having had time but he had helped capture a German mg at La Bassée. The CO winked at me behind the BG's back and Kearey, blast him, was grinning like an idiot. Then Cuthbert muttered something about getting the brigade's fair share of awards and we moved on. I somehow can't see me writing up Kearey for a DCM!

Afterwards we all marched past the Brig, played on by the band and drums. When it was over the CO ordered the officers to fall out and then told the RSM and SNCOs to march the Bn into their new billets in Nieuwkirke and the bugles to blow no parade for the rest of the day. He then told all the officers to lunch at the Mairie. CSM Rogers took command of the company and told me that Q Smith has been preparing figgy duff for the boys for their dinner. It seems he's scrounged some sugar and flour somehow. I don't know how he does it. Without the SNCOs we'd be lost. First mess we've had together since - when?

CO told us that the BG very impressed by the Bn and the spirit of the men. Lots of 'hear, hears' for that! Also told us that a big draft is on the way; 60 men, he said plus six officers, including Major Stockton as the new 2i/c. I know him from India when he was adjutant. Bit of a tartar but a good soldier.

Got a chance to catch up on the rest of the gossip. J. Hedley has a bad lung wound it seems, and was evacuated to Newhaven. Johnny Wybergh told me on the QT that the story of how JH got himself shot (as he put it) was all round the battalion.

Charles Berry very down. He tells me that B Coy is very shaky since the shelling and their losses at La Bassée. Henry was a popular OC and with CSM Jackson gone as well, it's almost like a new company. Over 20 dead and 50 wounded. Terrible.

Johnny Townsend (irrepressible as ever) took his "turban" off at lunch to reveal a neat scar on top of his head where he'd been grazed by the bullet. 'Centre parting from now on, chaps!' Typical Johnny.

Robin Hitchcock as mess president suddenly stood up and proposed the King. We toasted him in red wine and after that I had too much brandy and fell asleep. That's all we seem to do out of the line. Good day though. All officers billeted in the local hotel. Got a decent room and bed.

8 November

Damp day and late start. Good night's sleep. Found the coy at breakfast and all warned to prepare to move; 1 hour's notice. Nobody knows where. According to Richards it has all gone quieter up at Ypres. The signallers know everything! Even the guns rumbling in the distance has slackened off. Maybe it's all over?

9 November

Still in billets here at Nieuwkirke. Took the company for a short march this morning; just eight miles, and then ordered a make and mend afternoon. CSM Rogers crimed two soldiers for being drunk on parade. I'll deal with them at tomorrow's orderly room.

10 November

On the move again. The battalion had an easy march north to a place called Dikkebus just west of Ypres. Tented camp – astonishing! Company lines, company messing. Tents very old; mine has got 1899 on it – Boer War! Still at one hours ntm. All very quiet up here now. Wrote some letters. Will try and get into Ypres tomorrow to see what is going on.

11 November

(Written on the 13/14th): What a couple of days! Woken at 6.30 am by terrific bombardment to the north. Everyone stood to and by the time we'd had

breakfast ordered to move to Ypres. Waited all morning and then London buses arrived (16 men to a bus) and ferried us into the town. Debussed in the main square at a long wrecked building like the Houses of Parliament and then marched east out of town through the Menin Gate heading towards the firing. Lots of wagons, wounded soldiers pouring back down the road and even some stragglers. Saw some German prisoners in a cage. They looked pretty fed up.

Military Police checkpoints on the road directed us up the Menin Road until we got to a wrecked white château called Hooge (I think). Lots of shell fire up ahead and staff officers galloping up and down the road as well as wounded coming down. Noticed R.E.s lying in the fields either side of the road with rifles. Not a good sign! Asked an RE officer what was going on, told that he had been ordered to form a stop line with his men to block the Menin Road. Said that the Guards Brigade had broken. I couldn't believe that.

We deployed and waited there for hours. Then got orders to advance up the road. C coy was third in line and we were advancing by staggered pls on either side of the road. Lots of dead men and horses. Heavy shelling to our front and then we were halted and ordered to deploy left into some woods. Met a captain of the Ox and Bucks who had been hit by something. Couldn't see where but he was all dazed and almost incoherent. Kept talking about a place called Nun's Wood. They all looked the same to me!

About mid-afternoon I had dozed off in the field when Johnny Wybergh ran across to wake us up and telling us to advance in open order to our left front towards a wood. Passed a gunner battery firing their rifles! Their officer said they had no more shells.

I extended the company and moved forward by rushes towards the wood that Johnny had indicated was the objective. There was a lot of shot and shell flying and I saw men go down but we just ploughed on. I could see dear old D coy on our right, and then we really copped it. All kinds of fire hit us and I just shouted, 'Down! Take cover!'. I jumped into a new shell hole to find I was sharing it with an Ox and Bucks corporal and a private from the Sussex.

The O&B NCO was typical; cheeky. 'Hello sir,' he greeted me with. 'Nice to see that this is an all ranks shell 'ole!' He was firing out into the mist and told me that they'd just run into the Prussian Guard in the wood to our front and that they had driven them out in a bayonet charge. I tried to see the company but we were all pinned down. There was a lot of metal whizzing about. After a while as it started to get dark I walked down the line. Most of the soldiers were in shell holes and Meynell's platoon had quite a big group lined up in a ditch on the edge of a field to form a trench line. They were lying in water.

The CSM had organised a kind of HQ in a cellar beneath a wrecked building and we set up there. It had a table and some chairs which had been in the kitchen. Richards the signaller appeared and told me that he had been ordered to act as our coy runner as telephone lines wouldn't last five minutes in this. After a while Meynell appeared and asked for orders. I couldn't give any so just said hold on. Not very good I am afraid.

I sent Richards back to Bn HQ for orders and Belfield suddenly produced a brew of tea from the wrecked kitchen above. The CSM and I sat looking into the dusk drinking tea, watching the rain and listening to the shells and talking. Funny way to fight a war!

Behind us we could hear the dickens of a row but it really wasn't our battle. No orders – no idea! As it got more dark I walked down the platoons. The boys were fed up, wet and cold. Nobody knew anything and we were (in every sense!) completely in the dark. Told them to hold on. Silly order but what else could I say? The shells were still falling around us and there were burning buildings to our front. Everyone very windy, looking out to their front, not knowing where the Germans were exactly or what was going on.

Then the CO appeared. Asked us how we were and walked round the platoon positions with me. He is extraordinary; so calm and with a good word for everyone.

As we passed a tall hedge a voice in the dark said sharply, 'who's that?' It turned out to be Brigadier Fitzclarence of the Guards Brigade, who had lost his way. He and Colonel Birkin knew each other of old so we spent ten minutes in the dark while they yarned away. Extraordinary. Said they'd meet up for lunch at the Army and Navy Club when next in London! The BGen was trying to find some lost Grenadiers. Heard him say the Guards had been forced to dig in and stop the German advance earlier in the day and had many casualties.

Got back to Coy HQ and then the worst hailstorm I have ever seen rattled down for about 20 minutes. Terrible. At least we were inside. For the men lying out and in the open and the trenches it must have been awful. CSM said that the only consolation was that it was just as bad for the Huns.

By dawn it was obvious that the Hun push had fizzled out and Richards came with a scribbled note to pull back 500 yards and then assemble on the Menin Road at the bend down the slope. That took some time but we managed to fall in and call the roll. A lot missing, including the CSM. No one's seen him since last night. The Coy answered to 38 R & F and 2 officers, me and Meynell. 10 pl's Serjeant Ashworth told me that poor old Lt Miller had been killed in the night. Pity.

B Coy seemed bigger but I noticed A and D looked pretty thin too. Marched back down the Menin Rd to Ypres with shells falling behind us and assembled in the Grande Place where Daddy Harper the QM with the echelon was waiting with hot tea and

porridge, along with a lot of our walking wounded
(16, according to the doc) and stragglers.

We picked up another eight of C Company who
were being held in the corner by some MPs. Said that
they'd just got lost in the dark. Sjt Ledman of 9 pl was
with them and he'd brought them back as an organised
body, so I told the MP officer (who said they were
deserters) pretty smartly to shove off. Ledman
thanked me. Said the MPs had been stopping every
loose man on the Menin Road and making lurid
threats about being shot for quitting post and deserting
in the face of the enemy.

Just as we were leaving, Gen Haig, the Corps
commander, rode by in the square going up the line
with some staff officers. Immaculate horse, beautifully
turned out and with a 17th Lancer riding with his
pennant on a lance! Very calm, spoke to the CO and
saluted as we presented arms. Called back, 'well done
the Foresters' as he went off to the Menin Gate and
the front line.

Then marched back to Dikkebus, where I am
writing this in my tent on the 13th. Field kitchens and
transport arrived yesterday; kitchens 6.30 am and
transport about midday. Q Smith served every man
in the coy an egg and bacon plus a slab of bread dipped
in the fat for breakfast this morning and had put the
rum in the tea. Amazing!

We spent all yesterday getting cleaned up and
resting and some more came in, including Kearey who

told me that he had been knocked out (by a shrapnel bullet he thought) and had seen CSM Rogers patching up a wounded man forward of the Meynell platoon trench just before dawn on the 12th after the big hailstorm.

Kearey insisted on making me feel the lump on his head (which was pretty impressive) and told me some story about the MPs arresting him and marching him back to Ypres. I asked him what had happened and he just looked at me and said, 'Sure, I just escaped, Sorr.' Incorrigible!

Went over to bn HQ after lunch. New 2i/c Maj Stockton was there with the CO and Johnny W. I was about to leave when the CO told me to stay. Stockton still pretty much the same as I remembered him; tall and tough. The soldiers were scared of him in India but he was always fair. Remembered me and we all had a glass of wine before the other coy comds appeared. (CO had called a conference for 2 pm.)

CO briefed us that the battle had quietened down. The Germans had taken thousands of casualties (Charles Berry broke in, saying we haven't got off so lightly either, which earned him a few black looks.) But he's right. Johnny W told us that even with the latest draft the bn strength this morning was down to 390 r & f and 21 officers (that's with the 6 new ones.) We've lost a lot. A lot of officers especially. The pl comds cop it more than most others. Our own Miller from C., Hunter from A and Lester and Smith

*from B. Even Teddy Tulloch's off wounded. The mg
section is being run by Serjeant Lacey now.*

*The worst thing is the list of the missing. Doc
Dunn can account for 92 wounded out of the 420 we
had on the 10th, but that still leaves us really down;
ration strength of only 415 according to Daddy Tom
Harper, the QM, even with the new draft. Hardly a
battalion!*

*Maj Stockton queried the discrepancy between the
390 figure and the 415 figure given by the QM.
Daddy told him with a twinkle in his eye that "he'd
left a small margin in case some of the missing turned
up." The CO and the Adj looked at each other and
laughed. So that's how the QM does it!*

*Stayed behind and asked the CO what should I
do about the CSM. I hope to God that Rogers turns
up, but if he's been killed or wounded back there that
leaves C Coy without a CSM. CO said that best
thing was keep it in the Coy and appoint someone as
acting CSM until we knew for certain about Rogers.
There were good SNCOs in the other companies but
he was reluctant on campaign to peel them off from
their own companies. It was agreed that I'd move
CQMS Smith up. Noticed that Maj Stockton didn't
say anything- just listened.*

*As I left the 2i/c asked if he could call on the
company in the morning. 'Not to inspect' - he was
strong on that. 'Just to have a look around and get a
feel for the Bn.' Wonder what he wants? Said of*

course and told him we'd have coffee at 1100 am. Laughed and said he'd be there.

14 November

Odd sort of day. Cold and clear. Soldiers getting sorted out. Did Coy memoranda at 9.am. Only one of the drunk soldiers turned up. Asked Q Smith, who'd marched him in, where the other one, Bates, was and informed killed in action up near the Nun's Wood. Couldn't really press the charges against Tompkinson (his partner in crime) as CSM Rogers wasn't present. Q Smith piped up and said that according to Sjt Ashworth, Tompkinson had volunteered to try and get poor Lt Miller's body in and been told it was too risky. I listened gravely to all this and dismissed all charges for lack of evidence. However, I warned T. that I wouldn't be so soft next time and thanked him for trying to rescue Mr Miller.

Then a very odd thing. After they'd gone I told Q Smith to sit down and told him that I would be promoting him to Acting/CSM until Sjt Maj Rogers turned up or not. He got quite agitated. Told me that he didn't want promotion and was happy to stay on a Company CQMS!

I was astounded and asked him why. Told me that he likes being Q, was good at it and could do more for the coy than as the CSM. He's certainly an excellent CQMS, no doubt about that.

Said I'd take advice and dismissed him. Then Maj

Stockton came and walked round the coy. Talked to a lot of the soldiers, poked inside the tents, asked all sorts of questions. Remembered Kearey and Guard and Serjeant Doughty as a corporal from India. When we got back to the Coy HQ tent there was Q Smith waiting with steaming café au lait and a cake! It seems that they knew each other and had a good yarn. Was going to ask RS's advice about the CSM problem but held off. Upshot was he shook me by the hand and told me that C Coy was a model and I should be proud. Saluted and off he went.

Later. I went to see dear old Daddy Harper this afternoon in the QM's stores tent. He gave me a belt of whisky, puffed his pipe as usual. We yarned on a bit then he asked me what was my problem? (He said I only came to see him when I had a problem!) RQMS Slater faded tactfully away!

Told him about Rogers and Smith. He just grinned and said that he'd known Smith a long time, obviously he was happy as CQMS - out of the line, able to scrounge and get things fixed. Much more comfortable for him back in the echelon than going round the trenches under fire in the dark and the rain. 'He's not bloody daft, young Tommy!' What do you expect from a canny old soldier?'

I was a bit taken aback, to be honest. All that hadn't occurred to me. Asked him what should I do? Daddy was quite clear; keep him as CQMS and promote someone over him. What about Jack

Doughty, he asked? Must admit I hadn't thought of that. With his split service he was still quite junior. But with only two other SNCOs he's the only real choice within the coy. And he's a good man, no doubt about that. Told Daddy I'd sleep on it.

Gunn indeed appears to have slept on it and, according to other entries in his diaries, promoted Sjt Doughty to Acting CSM of C Company two days later, adding that the CO had told him, 'Good decision.'

CHAPTER 8

THE YPRES SALIENT, 20 NOVEMBER - 1 DECEMBER 1914

22 November 1914

We came out of reserve two days ago on the 20th and marched off to trenches at St Eloi. Not very far. Got a very cheerful send-off from the rear echelon. I begin to understand why CQMS Smith is happy to stay back out of it! Still no news of CSM Rogers. Company now has been beefed up to 102 R & F, A/CSM Doughty, 4 bandsmen as SBs and Richards and Morgan as signallers. Plus me, Meynell and the new officer, 2/Lt Brooks-Morgan. I've given him poor old Miller's pl and I've told Sjt Ashworth (who is a sound man) to keep an eye on him, and no stupid risks. The battalion's lost quite enough officers so far;

8 killed and 13 wounded since we came out in August. That seems a lifetime ago! Promoted Cpl Ruddock to pl sjt of my old pl. He seemed surprised but pleased.

The trenches are awful. Full of water half the time and it has become very cold. We relieved a regular RWF battalion in the line and they were glad to get out. They left some buckets with coke which they'd scrounged saying you'll need these. They were right. It is bitter.

The move up was quite good until we got to what they call a communication trench. Then we ran into all kinds of problems. At first the mud was only ankle deep, but gradually it got deeper and deeper as we went down the communication trench. Soon our heads were below ground level, and we were wading through icy water and mud. Overhead we could see the Germans lighting up the sky with flares; it's surprising how little you can actually see down in these trenches – just a narrow slice of sky above. I suspect that the Hun had got wind of our move and relief because soon he started sending some shells over. Luckily they just landed in the fields but we could hear their shrapnel whizzing around.

Just moving got more and more difficult. You had to pull every step out of the mud and pull yourself along just to keep going. Not helped by the fact that many of the boys were loaded down with kit: extra ammo, rations, water, even a coil of barbed wire. The upshot was that we were about an hour and a half late when we finally got to the RWF coy location. Their coy comd, Stockwell, was a bit sharp; greeted me with, "You're late!" Told him to blame the condition of the trenches, as he'd find out on the way home! He calmed down a bit after I'd offered him a belt from my hipflask.

CSM Doughty did a good handover of the stores with their CSM. Noticed that the RWF had a spare officer in Coy HQ as a 2i/c. Wish we did.

Shook hands with Stockwell as they filed out. They'd lost 1 officer (sniped) and 8 men in the last week and thought they'd got off lightly. Doughty started sorting the men out and after an hour I walked round the platoons to see that all was well for stand to. All seems to be in order, although the trenches in Meynell's part of the line on the left run down a slight slope and are flooded waist deep. There is actually a flooded ditch running forward through C Coy's line from the left straight into the Hun lines about 200 yards away.

Sloshed through the water and found Berry of B to make sure we were linked. Got a cup of hot cocoa with rum and he warned me that he's been told that there was lot of sniping going on. The RWF had had two offrs sniped last week, he said. Worth knowing. He said he thought that it was a dirty, cowardly underhand way to fight. Told him I thought that this was a pretty dirty war in every sense.

Got back for stand to. All quiet. Very, very cold and some drifts of snow blowing on the breeze. Called to an Orders Group for 9am at Bn HQ to make sure we've got our trench routine right."

23 November 1914

We are now in the trenches, and if this is soldiering then it's completely different from anything I've known. I think we are fighting the weather more than the Germans. It's bitterly cold and we are plastered with mud which then freezes, esp at night. Very hard to get rations up, let alone clean water. Told the pl comds to make sure all water is boiled (I know the men are taking water from the muddy ditch to make their tea.) Food is dreadful. We only have Army biscuits, cold bacon, bully and tins of jam in sacks to eat which we hang up to keep dry and out of the mud.

Just going round the pl trenches is exhausting. On the right they're pretty solid, although ankle deep in water. But poor old Meynell's lot on the left could be up to their thighs in water down by the ditch if we manned that last fifteen yards; it's a real weakness in our line. Kept the coy busy by making them improve their own dug outs underneath the parapet side and told them to dig into the wall above the water level. At least that way they stay warm from digging and can crawl into a funk hole if we were shelled or if they needed to sleep.

Doughty seems to have taken to being CSM like

a duck to water (and we've got a lot of that!) He gets round everywhere, works well with the pl sjts and watches over the soldiers like a hawk. I found him after morning stand to telling the pl sjts to make sure every man changed his socks every day to let the spare pair dry out, and to make sure that every soldier rubbed his feet until they were dry. Asked him why, and he told me that this is what they did down the pit if they were working in a waterlogged seam to stop the feet going all spongy. 'Like how your skin goes when you've been in the bath too long sir!' which made me laugh. A hot bath seems a very good idea!

Told the pl comds to inspect the men's feet every morning after stand to. Bit puzzled but explained why and they seemed convinced. Secretly, anything that forces the men to look after themselves and break up the awful routine of these horrible trenches is good.

24 November
On inspecting the left flank pl (9) after morning stand to, Meynell told me that he was sure that a German patrol had been spotted last night out in no man's land down by the ditch that joins the two front lines. That explains the sudden outburst of firing out there on our left last night. He explained that he put a sentry in the waterlogged trench for only 30 minutes at a time (because of the water) and Private Vernon opened fire down the line of the ditch when he heard a noise at about 3 am. Trouble is that the ditch is the boundary

between C and B coy. Unit boundaries are always a weakness.

Decided that we'd better send out a patrol after last light to work their way down the line of the ditch, lie up and see if the Hun really was out and about. Don't want him sneaking up on us in the dark. Briefed Meynell for the ptl, who called for volunteers. Vernon's hand shot up. I was a bit surprised and asked why so keen after last night; he replied, 'Begging your pardon sir, owt's better than another night standing up to your waist in freezing ******* water!' which got a big laugh. The whole pl volunteered! The men really are extraordinary. Told Meynell to fix it and brief me on the plan at coy hq later.

Briefed the CO when he appeared during the afternoon. He looked tired but insisted on going down the trenches and wading through Meynell's pl to move on to Charles Berry and B Coy on our left. Told me he'd get Johnny Wybergh to get a couple of the RA's guns on stand by after dark in case we needed some support.

25 November
Dreadful weather. Last night's patrol turned out to be quite exciting! Hugo Meynell led it – which made me furious, as we can ill afford to lose another officer. If he had told me I would have said no. However he took 12 men and they crawled out into no man's land after dark and laid up for a few hours. Then about two

o'clock they spotted a group of Germans coming towards them in the dark. Meynell says that they lay doggo in a big shell hole hoping that the Germans would pass them by. But someone fired from our trenches out on the right (A Coy!) and several of the Huns jumped into the shell hole to take cover! Apparently there was a bit of a melée in the dark with four dead Germans and Private Vernon bayonetted in the arm. The rest of the Huns fled but we were then subjected to half an hour's shelling and Pvts James and Murphy wounded. Pretty nasty. Three wounded in the trench as well and part of 11 pls parapet blown down.

It quietened down just before dawn when Meynell led a dash for our lines. I was there, as Doughty had told me what was going on and didn't think they'd make it. Sure enough an mg opened up when they started bolting for our trench but everyone got back in one piece except for Vernon who has now been sent to the Aid post. They flew in over the parapet like leaping gazelles! I don't quite know what to say to Meynell. I can either give him a good strafing or recommend him for a medal!

News came in during the morning that CSM Rogers has been officially posted 'missing, believed killed.' Terrible. He was a good man.

27 November
Terrible weather. Sleet, snow flurries. Cold - very cold

- and we are all tired. CO told me to put in three soldiers of the coy for an award. Talked to the pl comds and we agreed on Kearey, Vernon and CSM Rogers.

Very hard to write these things up as the old writing hand is half frozen and mud everywhere. Difficult for the diary, let alone writing decent citations for Brigade!

Ordered a wiring party for night after tomorrow. Decided to do nothing about the Meynell patrol as I feel I ought to go out myself later to see what no man's land is really like after dark. Should be interesting!

Told the CO and Adj, as we don't want any firing from A coy on the right (which is what started the ruckus last night.) CO says it is a good thing to go and have a look see, "but don't make a habit of going out on patrol – it's not a job for coy comds."

28 November (Written on 29ᵗʰ)

Interesting night! Set out with a section from 10 platoon (9 pl were out last night) at 11 pm on patrol. Sjt Ashworth in charge. Blackened faces, and minimum kit. Crawled out close to the line of the ditch and went forward straight towards the Hun lines. Took hours. Freezing cold and wet through. Huns popping flares up every so often – they have many more than us, obviously. About half way we could just see a bunch of Germans in the dark very quietly tapping fence posts in. Wire, I expect. Laid up and watched them from about 20 yards away. Ashworth sent 2 soldiers off to the left to crawl down into the ditch and try and go forward. It was full of water and we could hear them sloshing around. So could the Huns, because at one point someone said 'Wer ist da?' and walked forward to the ditch. The two men lay doggo and the Hun came back. We could hear a whispered conversation in the dark and then they went on working.

I was tempted to have a go at them but decided better to lie low and watch. Good thing we did, because after about half an hour a line of Huns we hadn't spotted suddenly stood up and advanced off to our right. We could see their bayonets in the dark. They stopped about ten yards to our right and then turned about and crept back to their lines, taking the wiring party with them. I swear I held my breath as they pulled back. Eventually crept back on our bellies; very cold, wet through. It took ages and we had to stop every time Huns put a flare up. Worst was crawling over the tumps that stuck up a little in no man's land - felt very exposed with backside in the air! The other nasty thing was crawling over dead bodies. Horrid. Hand squelching on a corpse.

Getting into the trench was not as straightforward as I had thought. First a nervous sentry (found out later it was young Thomas of 11 pl - we had swung too far out on our return crawl) who wasn't really aware that a ptl would be coming back. He challenged and I heard him cock his rifle, so shouted quite loudly, 'it's me, you damned fool! Captain Gunn. Don't you dare bloody well fire!' This shook him up and attracted Brooks-Morgan, the new 2/Lt. We had a hissed conversation at about 5 yards. Me lying flat on the ground and cross, him very nervous calling up from the trench. 'Is that really you, sir?' Farcical!

Then Jerry opened up with his mg and began to traverse our parapet. I tell you I lay low! We all did. After a while it went quiet and we slipped over the parapet like worms on our bellies to fall head first into the trench. Cold, tired, fed up and (if I am honest) not a little scared! Was going to give B-M a rollocking but the boy is new and I suppose that we all learned from the experience.

Found my way to Bn HQ where the CO, Maj Stockton and Johnny Wybergh were all up and waiting for me. Got a big mug of cocoa laced with brandy and recounted my tale. HQ dugout very warm and dry, thank goodness! Johnny plotted the patrol's route on his hand drawn trench map and the CO talked about getting more wire out and having patrols out every night to act as advanced sentries in case the Huns are planning any mischief. He told Johnny that he must send off a report to Bde HQ.

Before I left CO asked me what it was like. Told him about the conditions, cold, wet, jolly nerve-racking. He listened carefully then ordered that no more coy comds to go out on ptl and any offr going out but be cleared by him or the 2 i/c personally.

Got back to C Coy just before stand to and am writing this mid-morning in the Coy HQ dugout while CSM Doughty does the morning rounds and inspection for me. Thank God for Belfield, who had a piece of bread fried in hot fat with an egg (an egg!) waiting for me. Checked on the rest of the patrol and discovered that Q Smith was responsible and that every member of the patrol had been given the same and a double ration of rum. God knows how they do it.

CHAPTER 9

THE RAID

The CO's order that company commanders were not to go on patrol did not last long. Two days later, 4 Foresters were ordered by Brigade to mount a fighting patrol to collect intelligence on the Germans, ideally by taking a prisoner. Gunn appears to have either volunteered or been ordered to lead what was, by the standards of late 1914, quite a complex and hazardous operation. Presumably Lt Col Birkin felt that after his earlier experiences, Gunn and his company were best suited to lead such a raid. This early raid (1-2 December 1914) seems to have been one of Gunn's formative experiences on the Western Front.

* * *

Gunn was discovering that being an infantry company commander in the line meant a lot of work and very little sleep. Only two nights before he had led a patrol out into no man's land "to see what it was like" and now, as the dusk fell on a freezing cold November night, he was about to repeat the experience.

He finished briefing the officers and NCOs who would be taking part in the night's raid and told them to get some sleep before they set out at a quarter past midnight. Flurries of snow drifted into the trench as he turned into the company headquarters dugout, which was protected from the elements by a piece of sacking hanging down over the muddy entrance. He still had work to do. Inside was a makeshift table made from ammunition boxes and a piece of plank on which was a guttering candle and acting CSM Doughty, hands wrapped round a mug of tea. Belfield offered Gunn a mug. 'Going to be cold out there tonight, sir.'

Gunn nodded his thanks and turned his attention to the paper on the table. Doughty looked at him sympathetically. 'Battalion HQ are on our back, sir. Insisting that we get the citations off to them as soon as we can.'

Gunn surveyed the foolscap sheets. Writing had never been his favourite pastime and writing up accounts of half-remembered actions had been surprisingly difficult. He re-read his citation for Private Kearey's award and tried to remember the panic and heat of that September on the Morin. He closed his eyes and once again saw the French bridge demolition party… what had happened to them, he wondered? He saw again the Hussar and his horse shot down by the French, the anxious cavalry corporal, poor old Widdowson with a bullet in the stomach, bleeding inside and staying on to die, the desperate scramble up the slope to regain the battalion with bullets cracking all around them, John Hedley's stupid anger at the casualties ...

He shook his head. 'Do you remember that bridge down on the Morin, Sarn't Major?' He still found it difficult to call Doughty 'Sarn't Major' but that's what he was now.

'Yes I do, sir. Seems like a lifetime ago, doesn't it? At least it was warm then.'

'It's so difficult. These citations. They all deserve an award. How does one pick them out? I mean, Kearey; does he deserve it more than Ruddock? Or what about poor old Widdowson?'

Doughty rubbed his chin. 'Ruddock's got his promotion. That's a sort of award, isn't it?'

Gunn grunted.

'And Vernon's got his arm sliced open on that patrol. Bayonetted a German in the fight in the dark. That's worth summat, surely, sir?'

Gunn grunted again, shrugged and wearily signed his name at the bottom of the three sheets. Already they were muddy. Well, HQ will just have to put up with that, he thought.

'What did you put them up for, sir, if you don't mind me asking?' Actually Doughty knew very well what the three were being recommended for – he had taken the precaution of reading the drafts while Gunn was away earlier.

'Kearey a Distinguished Conduct Medal; Vernon the same; and young Humphries of Ten Platoon. According to Mr Meynell he went out twice into no man's land and brought

James and Murphy in after they were wounded. Damned plucky. That German machine gun was blasting away, if you remember.'

'Seems fair enough to me, sir. Pity we can't put CSM Rogers in for an award.'

'Don't think I haven't thought of that. But for what? Just being a damn' good serjeant major?'

Doughty was silent. Far off a gun fired, like a door slamming a long way away. They all waited until there was the unmistakable crump of a shell landing.

'How about this?' said Gunn and read out:

"For marked courage during operations in France, September until November 1914. This soldier showed noteworthy courage rescuing and helping his comrades at the Petit Morin on 13 September, despite a serious facial wound, and later at La Bassée on 16 October, where he was instrumental in silencing and capturing a German Maxim gun which had caused serious casualties to our forces. He has demonstrated utter contempt for danger and rendered great assistance to operations during the period under fire."

Doughty shrugged. 'Kearey?'

'Kearey; of course.'

'Sounds good to me, sir. But "serious casualties?" '

'I call killing a Brigade Commander a serious loss, don't you?'

Doughty nodded. 'Fair point.' He chuckled. 'You might add something like, "he, with his colleagues, has been a regular forager from our ally's farms and assisted the Quartermaster by providing the company with quantities of fresh food while on active service."'

Gunn looked at his serjeant major and smiled. 'Do you know, I'm not sure if that isn't a genuine attribute out here?'

Doughty grinned and looked around their muddy hole. 'I'd say it's essential, sir.'

Gunn looked across at Belfield curled up in the corner. 'Where's your dugout, Belfield?'

'One along sir. With Private Richards.'

'I need to speak with the serjeant major.'

'Certainly, sir.'

With great dignity, Belfield left.

When he had gone, Gunn rounded on Doughty. 'How are you getting along with Q Smith?'

'Fine, sir. No problems.'

'But he's much more senior to you?'

'I know that, sir. But he's happy to stay as CQMS. At least, so he tells me.'

'Why?'

Doughty rubbed his chin and seemed to come to a decision. 'May I have your leave to speak freely, sir?'

'Don't be so damn' silly. Of course you can.'

'Well. Speaking frankly, Q Smith likes being the CQMS. He is a rear echelon solder, and to be honest, I think he is happy to stay that way. Do you have any complaints against him, sir?'

'Not at all. Absolutely not. He's a first rate CQMS. I would say the best in the battalion, and C Company have always been well looked after. Extremely well.'

'There you have it, sir. He does what he does. Q Smith and I understand each other. There'll be no problem in C Company while we are working together.'

Gunn absorbed this in silence. A shell droned overhead from the German lines and exploded well to the rear.

'I hate those shells,' said Doughty, out of nowhere. 'You never know where they are going to land.'

There was a long silence. Gunn watched the guttering candle. Eventually Doughty said, 'Might I suggest, sir that you get your head down before midnight?'

Gunn grunted and pushed the citations to one side to reveal several flimsies underneath. 'What on earth are these?'

'Returns, sir. The RSM was telling me that battalion HQ has to render regular returns to Brigade now, as long as we're in these trenches. Some of them daily.' He watched for Gunn's reaction. He wasn't disappointed.

'Returns? We're supposed to be fighting a war, not filling in bits of paper like some pox doctor's clerk!' Gunn stared at them: "ammunition expended? Missing trench stores, viz, three spades, R.E,?' His voice rose; 'and what about this, "company crime sheets for October?" '

He looked at Doughty, who was smiling. 'It's not bloody funny, sarn't major! How the hell am I supposed to do all this and fight the Hun? Very well; ration returns I can accept…' He waved an arm, 'But we don't even have a company clerk!'

'Use Belfield, sir. That's what I'd suggest. He's an educated man, he's part of company HQ and he's not exactly over-employed. And I've already taken the liberty of telling the CQMS to let you have a daily return of rations and ammunition every morning, and I will do the daily strength and casualties. I do that anyway after stand down. Then all you have to do is check and sign them, sir.'

Gunn grunted. 'Makes sense. Thank you.' He sat in silence for a while. 'You're right, of course. Let's do as you suggest. It can become part of the morning routine after stand to.' He yawned. 'Oh well; I think I'm going to try and get some sleep.'

He went out and crawled into the tube-like dug out that contained his sleeping valise and a damp blanket, wrapped a muffler round his throat and quickly fell asleep. Within minutes the rest of the trench could hear him snoring. Belfield looked in and pulled Gunn's officer's great coat over the sleeping form. 'Out like a light, sir,' he observed to Doughty.

'Aye,' said the serjeant major. 'And he's leading a fighting patrol in four hours' time. Wake him at eleven, Belfield. You've got a watch, lad, haven't you?'

* * *

Promptly at eleven, Belfield woke Gunn and handed him a mug of steaming *café au lait*. Gunn massaged his face and looked around in the dark. It was bitterly cold and a hard frost. Shadowy figures could be seen manning the parapet. He stood shivering in the trench, hands clutched around the mug. 'Well done, Belfield. Where did you get this?'

'It was in your last parcel from home, sir, and you shared it out with me and the CSM. Remember?'

Gunn grunted assent. 'Well, thank you.' He burned his mouth and swore. Well, at least it woke him up. When he had finished he groped his way to the rudimentary latrine and began to prepare himself for the raid. He had little confidence in everything going right in the dark and confusion, and had deliberately kept his plan as simple as possible and with some extra safety precautions. After his experience of the other night, and having talked at length to Hugo Meynell, he was convinced that night raids would be very risky affairs and bound to take casualties.

When he had briefed battalion HQ on his plan earlier Major Stockton had queried his intention of putting out soldiers on the ground at regular intervals in no man's land with no other orders than to act as guides when the raid returned. 'Risky, don't you think? Is it really necessary?'

Gunn had shaken his head. 'It will be chaotic getting back. That's when we'll need clear guides, what with the flashes, shell fire flares going up, and casualties. We'll need every extra man, I'll bet on it.'

Stockton and the CO looked at each other dubiously.

'You don't sound very confident Gunn, I must say,' began the CO.

'Oh, I'm confident sir, never fear. I think we'll surprise their wiring party, all right. But that's just the start of it. There'll be a scrap in the dark, firing, mgs waking up, shells coming down and men getting hit. That's when we'll need the extra men to help us get back.'

Lt Col Sir Thomas Birkin nodded his head slowly. 'Well, if you say, so; I have to agree. And you've been out at night, which we haven't. It's your show and you must do it the best way you can. They're all volunteers, you say?'

'Yes sir. I'm using 12 platoon; they've been in reserve. They all volunteered. Every single man.'

'Remarkable! Well done, 12 platoon. Isn't that the one without an officer?'

'Correct, colonel. Hugo Meynell will be leading the observation party and Serjeant Maxwell will be leading his back-up sections from twelve.'

Gunn smiled grimly in the dark at the memory. He knew that Major Stockton would be there to see him off, as he knew that the CO and half the battalion would be waiting up to see how he got on.

He reached into his dugout and called for Belfield. 'Time to get started. Check my kit.' He handed over his personal belongings, some letters and a locket to his servant who wrapped them in a sandbag. Then, strapping on his revolver and making sure that he had a spare box of cartridges in his pocket, he turned to leave.

'Hang on sir,' said Belfield quietly, 'your face.' He produced an old cigarette tin lid and smeared a mixture of lamp black and grease onto his company commander's face. Gunn bore it stoically, muttering, 'I expect I look like a blasted nigger minstrel now.'

Tightening his belt a notch Gunn walked softly round the traverse to where the raiding party was assembled. With their assortment of soft woollen caps, balaclavas and blackened faces they looked a piratical crew, he thought as he went down the line, inspecting every man and making them jump up and down in turn to see if there were any give away rattles. Sure enough, two of the 12 platoon soldiers had tin boxes of cigarettes on them and were told to leave them behind. In the dark one of them said something and got a rasped, 'You won't be smoking out there lad,' from Serjeant Maxwell.

When he had inspected them Gunn told them to close in and reminded them of the plan.

'Right. It's now five minutes past midnight. In ten minutes we'll set out. Mr Meynell has already gone out with three men and is waiting where the Jerries were last seen wiring over the last few nights. They went out an hour ago. His job is to let us know if they are out again tonight. Now, for us, one section goes out over the left ladder and crawls one hundred yards and stops in all round defence. On the way you drop off a guide to lie up every twenty yards in a straight line. That's why you've got the extra men from four section. Two section you do exactly the same, but out on the right. Your section commanders have their bearings and when you eventually lie up you should be about fifty yards apart and one hundred yards out, if you've got it right. I expect you to be in position by one fifteen precisely. At that point I will be in the middle between you, with the snatch squad; that's three section under Serjeant Ledman.'

He drew breath. He had their attention, that he could see. 'At precisely one fifteen, Mr Meynell will flash his torch back towards our lines if – and only if - he has seen the German wiring party. The CSM will be watching. As soon as he sees me repeat Mr Meynell's flashes he will send up a flare to drop behind the German lines. That will illuminate the Hun working party from their rear. That's when Sjt Ledman and his squad will rush the Huns and grab a prisoner.'

He looked at Ledman, a stocky ex-miner from Chesterfield. 'You happy about that, Sarn't Ledman?'

'Oh aye sir. I'll go in wi' three of the lads; we've got clubs and bayonets, and rest of the squad are bayonet men. We'll bag thee one, never fear.' His teeth gleamed white in the blackened face

Gunn grinned back. If anyone could do it, boxing and tug-of-war champion Ledman could.

'Stout man. Now this is where it all turns on what happens next. Sarn't Ledman and his party leg it back as fast as they can, bringing with them at least one Hun. The rest of us cover that withdrawal and when I blow the whistle three times we crawl back along the lines of the guides lying out. The artillery have got a battery ready and will drop six shells into the Hun lines exactly two minutes after they see CSM Doughty's flare go up. That should keep the Germans' heads down as we pull back.'

He looked around. 'Any questions?'

'Yessir!' One of the figures in the dark stamped to attention. 'What happens if the Hun opens fire before that? If he spots us?'

'Then we abort. We stop. If we're rumbled, then we stop the raid and crawl back quietly and carefully. There'll be other nights. If you hear three whistles from then it's go home, whatever happens.'

Another voice said, 'What happens if Lieutenant Meynell doesn't flash his torch? If there are no Huns?'

'We lie up until 2.15. and them make our way back. Clear?'

CSM Doughty stepped forward and handed something to Gunn.

'What's this?'

'My bayonet, sir. Take it with you. It might be useful in the dark.'

'Don't be daft, man. What do I want with a bayonet out there? I've got my revolver.'

'And right noisy things they are too, sir. Just take it; just in case. It's sharpened like a razor.'

Gunn remembered that Doughy had spent a lot of his quiet hours sitting quietly sharpening his bayonet. The platoon joke was that he shaved with it. He took the eighteen-inch bayonet in its sheath, albeit reluctantly. 'Thanks Sarn't Major. I'll bring it back.'

An anonymous voice said, 'Aye. He'll need it for shaving in't morning!' to a splutter of laughter.

Dark figures loomed down the trench and a voice said 'Party, shun!'

Lt Col Sir Thomas Birkin's calm voice floated down the line. 'At ease, everyone. At ease. I just wanted to wish you all good luck and good hunting. He and the tall lean figure of Major Stockton loomed in the darkness. 'All well, Captain Gunn?'

'All well, Colonel. We're ready to go.'

The CO turned to face the raiders. 'I just wanted to wish you all the very best of luck. I am sure that it will all go well.' He saluted them. 'Go it, the Foresters.'

He turned to Gunn and shook his hand. 'Off you go, Tommie and be careful. Good luck!'

Gunn stammered a reply, then checked his watch. Twelve sixteen. 'We are one minute late. Let's go!' He climbed the trench ladder quietly, followed by his men.

* * *

Crawling across frozen tussocks in a Belgian field, thought Gunn, was a cold and miserable experience, as he inched in the dark towards a tump that was his objective – or was St Eloi in France? He couldn't remember. Christ, it was cold! His fingers were freezing.

Dimly he could see the shapes of his protection party, two riflemen from nine platoon who had volunteered to go out, 'as Mr Meynell and Sjt Ledman's out there too, sir.' He stopped crawling as a German flare fizzed up and burst, bathing the landscape in a wobbly silver light. Face to the ground he closed his eyes and waited for it to go out, but not before chancing a glance at his wrist watch. Just after one am! Well, they would soon be there.

By the time Gunn had settled on the back side of a low tussock about a foot high with Tancock and Noble, his two protection men on either side, he was aware of movement further out. He could just make out the dim shapes of Ledman's snatch squad off to his right. Further out he hoped that the two sections of 12 platoon were in place on either side.

The night was very quiet and still. Far off he could hear the occasional grumble of artillery to the north on the far side of Ypres, and he remembered the awful night when the Germans had nearly broken through. He tried to recall the date; 11 November – only three weeks ago? It seemed like the far side of the world. He shivered with the cold. Doughty's bayonet was digging into his side. He moved it to the small of his back.

He strained his eyes to the left towards the ditch and stream where he knew Meynell was lying up at his observation point. The Germans had been busy building a wire fence from the ditch across towards the centre of their front; every morning revealed it getting longer. They should be working just to his left front…

Suddenly he saw three torch flashes about 20 yards ahead in the dark and off to his left. He knew that Meynell would have his body curled round the torch to mask the light from the German. Three flashes! This was it. He swallowed hard, felt his heart beating and curved his body to hide his own torch from any lookouts to the front. Then, very deliberately, he flashed his own torch three times towards his own line a hundred yards behind. At first nothing happened and he wondered if something had gone wrong. Had Doughty not seen his torch?

He was just about to do it again when there was a pop and an arc of red sparks trailed up into the sky over their head. Just like Guy Fawkes Night, he thought. Then the flare burst with a louder pop, well over the German lines and he saw, clearly silhouetted, a dozen Germans working on their new fence about twenty yards ahead. They froze, knowing movement attracted fire. Out of the corner of his eye he saw Ledman and his men running forward, fast and silent.

They nearly made it. At the last second a German shouted, '*Achtung!*' but he was too late. The snatch squad burst into the Germans, who fled shouting. Some seemed to be engaged in a hand to hand fight with the shadowy raiders as the flare flickered and went out. For a second he saw a shovel raised and could hear swearing and shouting as the struggle for a prisoner was played out in the dark. A man screamed.

A single shot rang out; then another and suddenly all hell broke loose. A burst of machine gun fire ripped through the night. Gunn was aware of pounding feet as a cursing group of men swept by about ten yards to his right. Ledman? He hoped so. Flares went up from the German line and more shots rang out. Far off he heard the distant sound of doors slamming and knew that the promised artillery support was on its way.

Seconds later the line of the German trenches erupted in fiery red explosions. Gunn suddenly realised that one of the explosions had landed five yards behind him. He felt the heat of the explosion and heard the whirr of red hot chunks of metal whizzing through the night.

Shit! One of the British artillery pieces was firing short. Gunn pressed himself against the earth and quailed as another supporting salvo crashed down with at least one more shell well short and landing close by, in the middle of the raiding party, he thought.

Ahead, German machine guns raved and he could hear the cracking of bullets overhead as the Germans desperately traversed their fire. He blew his whistle loudly three times. That provoked another outburst of fire and, as he turned to crawl back, he distinctly heard the sound of the German guns opening fire in the distance.

He pressed himself flat on the ground as, with a noise like an express train, three shells thundered into no man's land. One of them landed only yards away. The stink of high explosive reeked in his nostrils. Flat on his belly he squirmed back and suddenly found himself sliding into a new shell hole in the dark. It was still warm from the explosion. The two soldiers with him slithered in seconds later.

'Fookin' 'ell!' observed a Derby voice.

'Quiet!' hissed Dunn. 'Who's that?'

'Tancock, sir.'

'Good man. Now keep your eyes peeled. Anyone see Serjeant Ledman?'

The Derby voice answered, 'Aye, sir. He went reet past me in't dark wi' a screaming Jerry. I think 'e's bagged one, reet enough.'

They lay in the darkness, as it seemed that every German was firing in their direction. Bullets cracked overhead and occasionally sent spurts of earth and stones flying into the shell hole. Gunn hoped that his men were inching back flat on their bellies. More and more flares sailed up from the German lines. He risked a quick peek over the edge of the shell hole. Nothing seemed to be moving. As he pulled back, another accurate German salvo crashed down around them. A large clod of earth landed on his back, and he cursed.

'What now, sir?'

'We'll try and crawl back. But watch out for Jerries and our own boys, some of them may have been hit.' He tried to think of something to cheer his pair up as another salvo thundered down making the earth shake under his stomach. 'Well, one good thing. We should be all right here for a while. They say that lightning never strikes in the same place twice.'

He saw the two exchange glances in the flickering light of the flares and smiled. Another salvo burst off to his right. He blew his whistle three times again and said, 'Now we've got to get back, boys. Stay close and stay low. Keep your eyes peeled.' He began to crawl out of the back of the shell hole as shrapnel shells suddenly burst overhead with their distinctive crack. He heard the lead bullets whistle and one of his protection pair say, 'Oh no!' It was Tancock, the one with the heavy

Derbyshire accent.

'What's up?' hissed Gunn.

'I'm hit, sir.'

'Where?'

'On me back.'

Gunn rolled back down into the shell hole. 'Where are you?'

Tancock rolled down against him in the dark with a bump. 'Sorry, sir.'

'Never mind that nonsense. Where are you hit?'

'Somewhere up in me back, sir. Right shoulder. A right thump. Thought I'd been kicked.'

'Let's have a look at it.' The German machine guns overhead went into a paroxysm of renewed stuttering. 'With that lot, I don't think anyone's going far just at the moment.' He switched on his torch. Down in the shell hole no one could see them, he reckoned. Tancock lay on his back, face contorted with pain. Gunn rolled him on his stomach and flashed the torch briefly on the injured Forester's back. Sure enough, high up on the shoulder was a small blood-stained tear.

'Noble.'

'Sir?'

'You keep a sharp lookout for Huns. I'm just going to patch your chum up.' Gunn ripped the jacket open with Doughty's bayonet. It really was razor sharp. Well at least he'd found a use for it. He revealed a nasty puncture wound in Tancock's back. It dribbled blood, but as Gunn watched he noticed that it was blowing bubbles. He pressed a first field dressing on the wound and bound it tightly round Tancock's shoulder. Calmly he said, 'Well, Tancock, you've got yourself a nice one there. Home for certain. How's it feel?'

'Not too bad, sir. It's kind of tight breathing, if you know what I mean.'

'I'm not surprised. I think you've been hit in the lung.'

'Is that bad?' wheezed an alarmed Tancock.

'Not nowadays. You'll live. Probably end up with a pretty nurse and a cushy posting to the Depot. Lucky chap.' Gunn prepared to put the bayonet back into its sheath.

Suddenly he heard the noise of running feet, a muffled curse and a body tripped and crashed into the shell hole from the British lines. In the dark it was hard to see what had happened but the runner fell hard on Tancock, who swore fluently as the unknown man crashed into his wounded back. Gunn and Noble tried to make out what was going on amid the thrashing limbs.

The smell was the first thing Gunn noticed. The running man smelled different. Then the collapsed runner shouted – in German. Gunn swung his elbow across where he thought the man's face was and got a hand in his own face for his trouble, the fingers scrabbling violently for his eyes. He reared back and, without thinking, pushed Doughty's bayonet as hard as he could upwards towards the noise. It crunched into tissue and he pushed and pushed as hard as he could. He heard a gurgling and felt warm wet blood, but still pushed. Suddenly the body went limp and rolled away, tugging the bayonet from his hand.

'Gottim, sir,' said Noble as the light of a flare revealed him kneeling and pulling his rifle back from the body to reveal a blood-stained bayonet. 'He's a goner. Where did he spring from?'

A new flare burst overhead. 'Blimey, sir, you've done for him yourself. Look!'

Gunn was sickened to see the German, hatless, horrified eyes wide open and blank in death, with Doughty's bayonet protruding from below his chin. 'You've spiked him through the brain, sir.'

Gunn pulled at the bayonet to retrieve it. The flares flickered out. He had to pull surprisingly hard before the bayonet came out reluctantly with a sucking sound that Gunn found disgusting. Tancock said weakly, 'Did you get 'im, Charlie?'

'Didn't need to, Tom. Mr Gunn 'ere spiked 'im through the 'ead! Fookin' brilliant!'

Gunn lay shaking with shock. The night had gone quieter and somewhere close by he could hear a man moaning in agony. He pulled himself together.

'Right, let's search this fellow. He's bound to have some useful intelligence, dead or alive.' The German's name turned out to be Otto Reinecker from Leipzig. Gunn bundled his meagre belongings into the German's small haversack and gave the sausage he found in there to Noble. German iron ration, he wondered? Tancock was breathing faster and weaker and Gunn asked him if he felt strong enough to crawl.

'I'll try, sir.'

He checked his watch by the light of the flares. 3.27. My God, where had the night gone? He rallied himself. 'Right, let's go. If you can't go on, Tancock, then say so, and I'll get you in.

All right? You go first. That way.'

They crept cautiously over the edge of the providential shell hole and began to crawl inch by inch towards the safety of the British trenches. About twenty yards out they came across the body of a Forester, mangled by a shell blast. 'It's Jake Shawcross sir,' whispered Noble.

'Leave him,' said Gunn, more worried about Tancock, who appeared to be coughing blood.

A shot rang out from the trenches in front and a bullet cracked by. Gunn saw the flash to his right and bellowed, 'Stop firing, you bloody fool or I will put you in front of a firing squad myself. It's Captain Gunn and I've got a wounded man out here, you idiot.'

'Sorry sir,' a muttered voice replied.

Inch by inch they managed to ease Tancock gently down into the trench to be met by anxious faces. Stretcher bearers quickly took him to the rear. Gunn's last words to them were, 'If you get stuck in a trench, take him over the top to the aid post. No delays. Understand?'

Then he sat on the fire step, dazed, and someone gave him a mug of steaming cocoa, well laced with rum. It was over. Someone shook his hand. It was Noble. 'Thank you, sir. For Martin. Martin Tancock. My mate. Thank you.'

He faded into the dark. CSM Doughty appeared. 'Thank God you're back, sir. We thought you'd had it.'

Gunn laughed. 'Nearly did, Sarn't Major. Nearly did.' They moved into the company HQ dugout. In the light he reached behind his back. 'Here. Here's a present for you.' He handed over Doughty's bayonet in its scabbard.

Doughty took it. 'Bring you luck, sir?'

'You could say that, Sarn't Major. Best have a look at it.'

Doughty unsheathed his bayonet and recoiled in disgust. The blade was bloodstained for all its eighteen inches and mixed with some traces of pink porridgey matter. Gunn hadn't noticed that in the dark.

'What happened?'

'A German ran into our shell hole. I stabbed him in the head.' He stared at the blade. 'That'll be his brains.' He shuddered. 'Right. I'd best see how the lads got on. Who got back? And then I'll have to report to battalion HQ. What's the score?'

Doughty pulled a face. 'You went out with 38 men sir, not counting Mr Meynell. We've only accounted for 28 up to now.'

It was Gunn's turn to pull a face. 'What? There's ten missing?'

'That's right, sir. No, make that nine. I wasn't counting Tancock.'

Gunn looked at his hands. 'Did we get a Hun?'

'Oh yes. Serjeant Ledman brought two of the bastards in. One made a bolt for it and escaped though, right on top of our trench.'

'No he didn't. I'll bet that's the one we killed. Trying to get back to his own lines. Fell into our shell hole.' Gunn smiled at nothing. Doughty realised that his officer was still in some kind of shock.

'The raiding party's assembled around the next traverse, sir. You'll be wanting to debrief them?' He picked up a hurricane lantern and led the way.

Wearily Gunn stood up and walked round the corner of the trench. By the dim light he could see a throng of dark figures, talking in low voices. Cigarettes glowed red in the night. A voice said, 'Here's the captain,' and the group fell quiet. Another salvo of German shells thundered down in no man's land.

'Well we've certainly stirred up a hornet's nest out there' asked Gunn. 'Have we called the roll?'

Both Ledman and Ruddock said 'yes' simultaneously. Ruddock's two sections had each gone out fourteen strong; the left hand section had three missing and the right hand section four.

'That's seven adrift,' said Gunn. 'Who else is missing?'

'Chilwell and Swain.'

Both had been in Serjeant Ledman's snatch squad. 'Chillwell's still out there', said a stressed voice. 'Some Jerry bastard stove his head in wi' a shovel.'

Gunn remembered seeing by the dying light of the flare a spade swung as the snatch went in. The voice went on, 'so I bayonetted the ******.'

The CSM looked up. 'Now then. Now then. Moderate your language, Spencer.' He was taking notes in his service pocket book.

Gunn finally pieced together the whole story. Everything had worked as planned. Ledman's squad had rushed the Germans, half of whom had fled and the rest put up a fight. Ledman had laid one out with a punch and Lance Corporal Newham had smashed another one to the ground and sat on him. In the confusion Ledman's men had bayonetted several of the other Germans. No one knew what had happened to Swain. Then Ledman had rushed his captives bodily back across no man's land and had almost got to the Foresters' trench when the Germans opened fire. They had all hurled themselves flat except Newham's German, who had taken advantage of the confusion to punch Newham in the head, wriggle free and sprint for the German lines - only to trip and fall into Gunn's shell hole.

'Where's the Hun prisoner now? asked Gunn.

'Back at battalion HQ by now, sir.'

Gunn turned his attention to the two cover sections. It seemed that everything had gone smoothly until the supporting shell fire had started. The right hand section had then been hit by the British shell dropping short. It had either killed or blown up four of the party and wounded two others, including Corporal Newton, the section commander. The party had only been able to get back because of the four extra soldiers lying out in no man's land who had acted as stretcher bearers and dragged the wounded men back.

'How bad were they?' asked Gunn.

'Bad enough, sir. Nasty shrapnel wounds.' It was one of the soldiers who had been posted as a guide. 'I brought him in. Corporal Newton, I mean. He'd been hit by one of them copper driving bands from a shell, across the legs. The thighs, at the back. It was still in there. We thought it best not to pull it out.'

'How did you get him back?'

'I thought fook it, and just carried him back on my back. We were lucky.'

He was from 12 platoon, thought Gunn. Fletcher. That was his name. Always in trouble back home, according to Doughty; yet here, as steady as a rock. War was bringing out some big changes as it exposed true character.

Out loud he said, 'That was a damn' brave thing to do, Fletcher. Well done.'

'Probably saved Newton's life, sir,' chipped in the CSM. 'He was bleeding bad.'

The left hand section had a similar tale, except that they knew that one of the group had been caught by a machine gun burst as he stood up to try and dash back amid the shell fire. The Section Commander, Corporal Shelton had seen the body of Private Wallis. 'Blown into bits. A shell,' was his laconic confirmation. No one knew what had happened to the other missing man, Tait.

Finally Gunn raised the thought that was on everyone's mind. 'So who's still out there?'

The Serjeant Major closed his notebook with a snap. 'Mr Meynell and his two, for a start. They should have been well back by now.' Gunn glanced at his watch. It read 4.58. 'Can we risk going out to look for the missing?'

The CSM shook his head decisively. 'I wouldn't risk it, sir; Jerry will be well on the lookout now and we've not got that much dark left. And the CO will be wanting your report.' He handed Gunn a page from his notebook. 'Here's the numbers, sir.'

Gunn took the page absently. 'What about your notebook?' he found himself saying. Doughty looked at him, puzzled. 'I've got a carbon in my notebook, sir.'

'So you have.' Gunn got wearily to his feet, thrust his mug into someone's hand and lurched off down the trench. At the corner traverse he stopped and looked back. 'Bloody well done, chaps. All of you. I'm proud of you and I'll make damn sure the CO knows. Thank you all. Now get cleaned up and be ready for stand to.'

What Gunn didn't know as he staggered off to report, was that unknown to everybody, Private Kearey was crawling through the night looking for the source of the moans he could hear in no man's land. Just before dawn and halfway across, he located it. It was Private Tait, crawling weakly through the freezing grass and mud, minus his left leg from the knee down.

'Saints preserve us,' muttered Kearey.

Tait opened his eyes. 'Hello Paddy. I've lost me leg.' He started to cry. 'I'm so cold.' Kearey peered at the stump in the dark. It wasn't bleeding much and he wondered if the red hot shell splinter had sealed the blood vessels.

'Niver you mind, Tommy Tait. We'll be getting you back now to a nice warm, comfortable hospital bed. Now tell me, does it hurt much?'

Tait shook his head. 'I can't feel it. It's buzzing more.'

'Right, now.' Kearey looked around. The palest streak of dawn was low in the east. A German machine gun spat a burst into the dark. He could see the flashes off to his right. He came to a decision.

'Tait, me old darlin' I'm going to drag you back. Now I want you to lie on your back. I'll wrap your legs together first and you help me if ye can. Pull with your arms like a good feller.' He put a first field dressing on Tait's stump and made sure the bandage went round both legs. The he grabbed Tait's shoulder straps and lying on his back, inch by inch heaved his half-conscious burden across the frozen ground. It was hard work and despite the freezing grass he was soon sweating with effort.

After they'd gone about half way Kearey stopped for a breather and realised that Tait had lapsed in unconsciousness. He also noted with alarm that he could already dimly make out the outline of the British parapet. The light was growing. With the strength of desperation and regardless of the noise, he dragged the unconscious man nearer to his own lines.

The final ten yards were the worst. An anxious voice called out, 'Halt! Who goes there? Halt or I fire!'

'Will you shut your racket, ye eedjit? It's me, Paddy Kearey and haven't I just got poor Tom Tait with me? Help me, because he's hurt bad.' He dragged himself to the single line of sandbags that marked the edge of the trench. A worried looking row of faces looked up at him and Kearey saw that the trench was fully manned for the morning stand to.

'Get me a rope, you fool.' The startled sentry brought a coil of rope from a dug out. Kearey crawled back to Tait and looped the rope underneath his armpits. The he crawled back to the edge of the trench and heaved the man towards him. When he had hauled Tait to the sandbags he flung the rope into the trench and rolled in, to fall with a crash on the frozen mud below.

'Jesus and all the saints,' he was cursing when Serjeant Ashworth appeared down the trench.

'What the hell are you up to, Kearey?' he began.

'Bless you serjeant, darling,' panted Kearey. 'Will you just pull on this rope and together we'll get poor old Tommie Tait in to the trench. He's lyin' unconscious up there, so he is.'

An astounded Ashworth risked a glimpse over the parapet to be confronted by the sight of a mud streaked and very pale Private Tait lying a foot away from his face. He jumped down and joined Kearey on the rope as they heaved the body over the edge until it was half in. Then willing hands lowered Tait gently to the floor.

A voice shouted 'Stretcher bearers!' as Kearey untied the rope and sat panting on the floor of the trench. He looked up at Ashworth. 'Well, I'd best be getting' back to me post, Serjeant, for they'll be missing me for sure.' He stood up and walked stiffly down the line towards 11 platoon.

Gunn's diary concludes the story. His total entry for the raid runs to three closely written pages, one of his longest entries for the period.

He was obviously deeply affected by the sights and sounds of the raid and was genuinely concerned for the welfare of his soldiers. The last part of the entry reads:

> *2 December (Written 3 December 1914)*
> *After I'd seen the raiding party I reported to bn hq. It was just about dawn but they were all waiting for me. When I walked in they all stared at me in horror. 'Are you hurt ?' said the Colonel. Then I looked down. My tunic was drenched with blood. It must have come from the man I had stabbed with Doughty's bayonet. I was so tired I just laughed.*

They gave me a mug of cocoa which was stiff with something (the colonel's brandy, I think!) and I went through the story. They listened, Maj Stockton was taking notes as well as Johnny. I ran out of steam half way through and they sat looking at me as if I was an idiot. Fortunately a runner suddenly appeared and told us that Private Kearey had not deserted but had brought the wounded Private Tait in from no man's land. I didn't quite understand this but they all relaxed and Johnny W went off to write up some report for Brigade.

CO shook my hand and said that Maj Stockton would cover C Company's stand to that morning. Must admit I was too tired to care.

Dunn, the doctor, appeared covered in blood and told us about casualties. Not very good. Seemed surprised to see me. Said something about he'd heard I had been killed! Rubbish!

Colonel very insistent on how I was so sure that the Royal Artillery had caused our casualties. Told him that I heard the first six rounds land and one of them was right in our midst. Doc Dunn chipped in that the copper driving band he pulled out of poor Cpl Newton's thighs had definitely been an 18pdr shell – so must have been ours. CO looked very upset and wondered how? Maj Stockton told him that some of the RA's gun barrels were very worn and needed replacing. I didn't help by saying that the gunners were often called the 'Dropshorts' by the men. I could see the CO didn't like that.

Terrible night. Still no news of Meynell and his pair. Didn't wash and got my head down after the dawn stand down. 2i/c came by but told him I would stay on duty.

3 December 1914

Apparently, Kearey went out without orders last night according to Sjt Ashworth and brought Pvt Tait in, badly wounded. The more I see of Kearey the more I realise that the man is a brick. I don't care that he drinks and gambles when he can. Kearey is a real soldier. Not like some.

Asked CSM Doughty what he thought. He smiled and said 'I'd make him a platoon serjeant, sir!' Very funny. But he may be right, that is what so difficult about this war. Things are turning on their head.

For example, heard yesterday that the Regimental Police Serjeant, Willcocks, a great battalion boxer in peacetime (and a nasty bully too) has been shipped back to England with 'nerves!'

Still no news of Meynell. Terrible. C Coy officers are down to just me and young Brooks-Morgan.

Relief tomorrow, thank God! 19 Brigade will be stood down and pulled back into reserve, according to the CO. We are handing over to 1ˢᵗ Hampshires from 11 Bde at midnight.

Spent the day clearing up and getting the trench shipshape for relief. We are all very tired.

CHAPTER 10

A BREAK FROM THE LINE - DECEMBER 1914

The Foresters were pulled back and relieved the next day. As the fighting at Ypres died down and the weather got worse, some kind of routine began to assert itself. Both sides tried to make themselves comfortable for winter.

> *6 Dec 1914*
>
> *Back out of the line, thank goodness. The relief went well but we were strafed as we came back. Heavy bombardment and Colonel Birkin wounded by shell splinter as they cut across the open ground, according to Johnny W. Bad news.*
>
> *C Coy got off lightly. Two men from Sjt Ruddock's 12 pl hit by shrapnel, one on the head, another in the shoulder. They'll live.*
>
> *Bad business about the CO. Got into billets at*

Kemmel in the dark and told by Doc Dunn that poor Tait (the man Kearey brought in from the raid) had died. Loss of blood apparently. Pity.

CQMS Smith had a hot plate of stew, fresh bread and gallons of hot tea waiting for the coy. Marvellous. Offered second helpings as he had lashings left over. Explained that the Company now down to 58 effectives: 58! A whole company! And he'd cooked for 100. Checked the boys are all bedded down (on straw, of course) in their barns, made sure we had sentries out, and then curled up in a corner of an abandoned cottage by the old iron stove which Belfield had got going. We are all so tired. No more tonight.

7 December 1914

Make and mend. Ordered a clean up day. No parades, just get ourselves sorted out and tidied up. Walked round the coy – or the remains of it! And tried to talk to every man. New draft arrived. C coy gets 30 rifle and bayonet men, 2 corporals and a Serjeant Butterey, who I had met at the Depot before the war broke out just as he was being discharged for his pension! He remembered me and I think he is a bit shocked at what he finds. Did most of his time in India and South Africa. Doesn't look happy!

8 December

Not much to write. Called the SNCOs at noon

together with young Brookes-Morgan, who looks like becoming a first-rate subaltern, to discuss the raid. In the middle of it Maj Stockton (who is now acting CO) appeared and asked what we were doing, a bit sharpish. I explained that we were trying to learn some lessons from the raid. He asked if he could join us, sat down and listened. Main lessons seem to be that our own artillery support caused the worst confusion by dropping short and we'd have done better without it. And we needed SBs well forward plus white tape on the ground to guide us back. Everyone agreed that raiding was dangerous and that casualties were inevitable.

Maj S said at the end 'who carried the wounded in?' Told him Fletcher and Kearey. He stared at me, and I knew what he was thinking. When I had told the others to fall out, he said quietly, 'those two have some of the worst crime sheets in the battalion!' I agreed but said that the war was bringing out some new opinions as to who were really the best soldiers.

*We then had a chat about the men. I told him that they were mostly different from the regulars I'd seen in India with the First battalion. Maj S. agreed and puts it down to the fact that the 4*th *is an old Militia battalion. So the men are different. A real mix of old soldiers, militia waiting to leave the service or to join into the Territorials, reservists and people like me back on leave or on the Depot strength.*

Told me that dear old Hobbs had actually pinched

about 40 of the keener civilian volunteers who had been queuing at the Depot back in August, signed them on as Territorials on the spot (!) and posted them straight into the battalion as it was forming, to make up the numbers for the War Office! Very naughty! Maj S laughed and said 'hope Kitchener never finds out we've poached some men from his 'New Army'!'

Apparently poor old Hobbo called it 'puttying up the new battalion' and insisted that they could learn soldiering best from serving with an active battalion, not training on Salisbury Plain. I agree. At least he leaves some legacy, because these new men (and we've spotted them) are shaping up well.

Maj S adamant that this mix of men makes for a completely different way of thinking from many of the old regulars. The men are genuinely keen. He thinks it makes for a better bn all round.

Still no news of Meynell. I may have to write his people back home. Hope that he turns up.

8 December

Very cold now. Snow flurries and sharp frost. Sent Sjt Butterey to 11pl as no offr or SNCO. He seems happy enough. I'll need to keep an eye on him though.

At the CO's conference at noon, Maj Stockton told us that we are due to go back into the line next week, that the Colonel is recovering back in England and that John Hedley and Teddy Tulloch are on the mend as well. Also told us that RSM Booker and RQMS Derbyshire have been sent back to England to be commissioned as 2/Lts!! Amazing.

New RSM is to be Housely (from B coy) and CQMS Hammond from A is the new RQMS. We really are seeing some changes.

These changes were hardly surprising. The BEF had lost 89,864 men killed wounded or missing since August, most of them among the infantry battalions of the first seven divisions, which had started out with 84,000 men! Losses among officers and senior NCOs were the most serious. Many surviving SNCOs were sent back from the BEF, either to be commissioned or parcelled out as trainers among the teeming amateur battalions of Kitchener's New Armies back in Britain.

The German losses against the BEF are hard to quantify. Germany lost 500,000 men in the first five months of the war; of which 134,315 are admitted during the Ypres battles; but the French fought at 1st Ypres too. Adding the numbers of casualties during the August retreat from Mons, the Marne and on the Aisne, the BEF probably accounted for about 150,000 Germans during the campaigns of 1914. No one can tell for sure.

The scale of the losses horrified everybody. No one had expected such numbers and the medical services of all the combatants were overwhelmed initially. Industrial warfare was wreaking havoc on an unheard-of scale, artillery in particular. Where in the Russo-Turkish war of the 1870s artillery had accounted for only 2.8% of the casualties, by early 1915 modern guns were causing 58% of the BEF's total.

The 4th Foresters had suffered grievously since August. Of

the original establishment of 970 men and 30 officers who had set out for France, they had lost 203 killed or missing, plus 452 wounded in action: a total of 655 casualties. Only 15 of the original officers had survived; 9 had been killed and 6 wounded. This 50% loss of officers and 60% casualties overall would have serious consequences in the months and years ahead, as a new BEF tried to learn its trade from scratch.

To take just one example, 7 Division, which arrived during October, were pitched straight into 1st Ypres, losing 9,000 men and 364 officers. Individual units reflected this heavy toll. The 1st Battalion of the Black Watch (official battalion strength, 1,000 all ranks) was down to one captain and 309 men. 2nd Grenadiers had lost their entire strength by December 1914: 32 officer casualties, 739 other ranks killed or wounded and 188 men missing. These dreadful casualties ripped the guts out of the pre-war Regular Army.

One of the worst results was the loss of properly-trained staff officers. Of the British Army's 960 trained staff officers on 4 August 1914, at least half had been killed because the majority had 'wangled' postings back to their parent regiments to join in the fighting – and become another casualty. This lack of properly trained staff officers would have serious consequences for the BEF over the next three years.

Brigadier General Lord Cavan, who took over 4 Guards Brigade in mid- November 1914 perhaps best sums up the BEF's extraordinary achievement:

No words can ever describe what the devotion of men and officers has been under trails of dirt, squalor, cold, sleeplessness and perpetual strain of the past three weeks. We (4th Guards Brigade) arrived 3,700 strong, go back about 2,000, but to my mind nothing finer was ever achieved by men.

It is hard for us, looking back, to realise that no one at the time quite grasped that trench warfare – effectively one huge static siege dominated by artillery – was going to be the new form of warfare. Soldiers and generals alike were baffled by the way the war had turned out. The French general Foch complained that he was 'fed up,' having been sent to Artois to a campaign without flanks. 'How can I manoeuvre?' he grumbled.

The Polish economist Bloch's pre-war prophecy, 'in the next war the spade will be as important as the rifle,' had come true.

But as the Foresters prepared to go back into the line they little knew that they would be witnesses to one of the strangest and most poignant events of the First World War – the Christmas Truce of December 1914.

CHAPTER 11

THE CHRISTMAS TRUCE

The Foresters went back into the line at Frelinghein, just north of Armentières, on 15 December 1914. They took over trenches from covering the front near Teiturer. Gunn's diary takes up the story:

15 December 1914
Marched to a place called Teiturer (I think) and took over trenches from 1st East Surreys under B-G Rolt, 14 Brigade. As dawn broke we could see that it was not a healthy spot and within an hour we had our first casualty – Parkin, sniped. He had been working the pump at the low end of the trench (which was flooded because of the thaw) and stood up straight to complain about something, according to his mate on the pump. Crack! Shot through the head. From somewhere off

to the right, according to Pvt Guard who was there. The men are very upset about this and threatening all kinds of vengeance if they get their hands on a Hun sniper. They think it's 'unsporting'!

These trenches are badly laid out because the Huns can catch us in enfilade where our line bends back almost at a right angle. Suggested to Maj Stockton that we pull back about 100 yards in the middle to straighten the line. He just looked at me and smiled. 'You're probably right, Gunn,' he said. 'But the BG would have our guts for bootlaces if we gave up so much as a yard of trench.'

So that's that. I think it's an unnecessary risk but orders is orders. Not happy. Told the boys to build up the parapet at the danger spots. Very cold and looks like a hard frost on its way.

Otherwise, this is a quiet position. The other good thing is that our rations come up regularly and plentifully. There a sunken road behind the battalion and a deep communications trench leading straight into our company forward position. That means that Q Smith can get hot food up after dark, which he does, much to our delight. The other companies not so lucky I think.

Their problem was that they don't have a good comms trench like us and that the Hun is using searchlights from behind the lines at night. Patrolling into no man's land is out of the question. However Charles (Berry) of B coy tells me that there were *always plenty of volunteers for the rationing parties, as they had first go at the rum, cigarettes, etc.*

17 December
Really cold today and some snow on the ground. We have a sniper out to our right front. He has had a few goes today and finally managed to hit poor old Brooks-Morgan in the shoulder as he was checking his platoon this morning. The boys are very angry and threatening revenge. B-M was a good and popular officer. Gone back down the line and back to Blighty, I suspect. I am now the only officer in C Coy!

19 December
A curious day. The CSM came to see me after stand to and said three of the soldiers had requested a formal company commander's interview. Very odd! Asked him what about and he just rolled his eyes. Eventually Kearey, Guard and Fletcher appeared. Caps off; very proper. Quite ridiculous in a mud hole of a company HQ on a freezing cold day, but that's soldiering out here.

I was quite crusty and regimental, but they told me they wanted to go out and find the sniper. All three are marksmen (Guard is the company's best shot) so I looked for guidance at CSM Doughty. He explained they wanted to go out well before dawn and lie up to see if they could see anything.

I was doubtful, but Doughty said he thought it

was a good idea. I went along with it and they cheered up and went out q. excited. CSM says it would be good for the coy. Can't do any harm. Can it?

Told Johnny W and Maj Stockton at CO's conference about the three musketeers and they just shrugged. I think perhaps we in C Coy take this sniping business too seriously?

21 December

I was wrong about the sniping.

Two men were sniped in A coy (on our right) yesterday. Robin Hitchcock furious and wanted to set out himself to "bag the blighter" as he put it. He's shot tiger in India so thinks of it as just another hunt. Told him of our three and waited all day for results. Nothing, except the sniper had a go at us about 3 pm, just missing Hardy of 11 pl. Then about 4 pm just as it's was getting dark heard two shots and about an hour later our trio rolled into the trench claiming that they had shot the sniper. He had been hiding under an old garden gate not 100 yards from our lines. Told 9 pl to blast it with 5 rounds aimed fire just to be sure. Caused the most frightful wind up from across the way! Jerry mgs still rattling away.

Told Maj Stockton, who later told me he had asked for a bombardment on the ruined farm cottage about 200 yards away to our right tomorrow as he was certain that was the Huns' main sniper nest.

21 December

Today at noon we got 18 rounds from the RA at the farm. Blew it to bits. No more sniping! Told CSM to say well done to 'the three musketeers'. Maj Stockton talking about nominating two snipers from every coy. Good wheeze.

22 December

Dreadfully cold. No news of relief. Some Christmas parcels from home as the post arrived. Seems that father has been counting up the number of officers killed from the list in The Times. Says it's very serious with several thousand names! Got Christmas card from Dorothy and parcel from Mother with green sock, green muffler, some cigars and one of her cakes.

23 December

Trouble. A member of 12 platoon has been shot in the hand. Odd business. Acting Sjt Ruddock has crimed him for a self-inflicted wound and the CSM has been doing a little quiet devilling. It seems to be true. Spoke to Doc Dunn when I visited the RAP afterwards to see what had happened. Barraclough started crying. He's from the last draft and only a young lad, just 18 and according to Sjt Ruddock, a bit soft. The boy virtually admitted he'd done it himself. Doc Dunn wouldn't commit himself. Went to talk to Johnny W. about this, when Maj Stockton came in and said, 'charge the bastard. If we don't, they'll all think there's a soft way out of the line.' So he has been charged with a self-inflicted wound. Theoretically it could be a capital offence. Not a happy day.

24 December
Christmas Eve. I had hoped that we would be relieved in the line but no news from Brigade, apart from a string of complaints that we haven't put accurate ration returns in! One good thing. At the back of our trench line is a wrecked farmhouse. It had been shelled to pieces and is pretty derelict, but the CSM came to see me after this morning's stand to inform me that there was a wine cellar down there. Apparently Kearey (who else!) had gone scrounging in the dark and fallen into the cellar. Dozens of bottles of good wine were still there. CSM asked me what to do. Told him not to be daft; count it, guard it, and give every man a bottle as a Christmas box.

25 December 1914
This has been the most extraordinary day! We knew that something was up because the Germans opposite had put little fir trees with candles on their parapet last night on Christmas Eve. It was very still and cold and we could hear them singing. Recognised Silent Night. Beautifully sung. Was a bit perplexed as to what to do. Our soldiers joined in the carols and I could hear them shouting 'Happy Christmas.' Could hardly tell

them not to. Spent half the night up. After dawn stand
to and breakfast (bacon and bread) there was a lot of
shouting. The boys told me to come and see. It was
very foggy. Risked a peek over the parapet and there
to my amazement was a blackboard on the German
trench with 'Happy Christmas' on it! There was also
a tall German officer walking across no man's land,
bold as brass, hands in the air. He had stopped in the
middle, shouting in English, 'Happy Christmas to the
Sherwood Foresters!' and then, 'Come and see.'

Sjt Ruddock said, 'shall I shoot him sir?' Told him
not to be so damn' silly and clambered out of the
trench. Slowly! Must admit it felt strange to be
standing up in the open. Like being naked. Was a bit
windy, to tell the truth. Anyway he called me over
and waved something. I went over and he produced a
silver cup and a hip flask and offered me a glass of
brandy. Ansbach he called it. Very good on a cold
morning. Then he pointed to my Webley and said that
I wouldn't be needing that today. Felt a bit
embarrassed to be honest. He flipped the strap on his
empty leather holster; he was completely unarmed.

Didn't know quite what to do and shook his hand.
He was a tall fellow, quite smart, with a beautiful grey
greatcoat and a smart hat. I must have looked a sight,
unshaven, covered in mud, no hat and with a green
muffler round my neck. I saw CSM Doughty looking
out at me from our lines shouting 'What does he
want?' so asked the Hun did he want anything. He

just said, 'Ja! No shooting today,' and waved his hand. Suddenly his soldiers started climbing out of their trenches, all unarmed and before I knew it the ragamuffins of C Company were climbing out and walking across no man's land to meet them.

It was an extraordinary sight in the mist. The soldiers were standing there all mixed up, talking as much as they could, shaking hands and swapping cigarettes. Then Doughty appeared with a bottle of white wine from the farmhouse, came up, saluted very formally and said 'I thought you might like to offer the gentleman a drink at Christmas.'

I was flummoxed! Before I knew it one of the Huns produced a corkscrew, a German soldier brought some glasses (I found out later he had been a waiter in the Strand before the war!) and the Hun and I were toasting each other in the middle of nml, while the soldiers on both sides cheered themselves hoarse. I was worried that we might be in trouble but looked over to A coy and could see a crowd milling about in front of their lines, too.

Didn't quite know what to do, so told the Hun that I would return to my dugout and remove my pistol. He clicked his heels and bowed, and said he had a gift for my men. Got back to our trench – deserted! to find a very agitated Maj Stockton demanding to know what the hell was going on. Explained and told him to see for himself. He looked out and like me at first he could hardly believe his eyes.

I could see that he didn't know what to do either. 'I can hardly open fire sir, can I? I remember saying. He was stumped, so I said, 'why not come and see?' He shook his head and went off to bn HQ.

When I got back to the meeting line I discovered the Germans had produced a barrel of beer which they broached and offered to our soldiers. CSM Doughty offered to try the first mess tin to check it was all right, which got more cheering from the boys, then they all tucked in.

The officer, who introduced himself a Senior Lt Freiherr von Marburg, told me that his soldiers all came from the Rhineland and were fed up with the war. I had to agree. He told me the beer came from a Belgian brewery about a mile back behind their lines which was still in operation. I offered him one of my good cigars and we stood there smoking and blowing smoke rings while the men talked and mucked in together while someone even organised a kick about game of football!

We agreed not to fire, not to go too close to each other's trenches and parted with mutual salutes. I went back to our trenches to smarten myself up and met Johnny Wybergh trudging down the line heading for B Coy on our left. I told him he would get there quicker on top today. He just rolled his eyes and said that Brigade had demanded a report on what was going on. He looked over the parapet, muttered 'Good God!' then slowly climbed out. He was shaking his head in disbelief, but he disappeared walking down to B coy's lines on top of the trench line.

The rest of the day passed much the same. Q Smith appeared in the middle of the day with a ration party and hot dixies. 'It's the lad's Christmas dinner sir,' he greeted me. He looked out at the scene and took his hat off to scratch his head. It was really rather funny. 'We're supposed to be slaughtering each other, not playing football, sir,' was his verdict, which was quite good, I thought. He said he'd managed to save a tin of Maconochie's meat and veg stew for every man along with potatoes and figgy duff. He had plenty of grub and it was hot.

I told him to take the ration party out into nml and share out what they'd got. I noticed he'd also got a SRD jar of rum, so I told him to share it out among the soldiers on both sides. 'It's only about three quarters full,' he admitted. I must have looked at him, because he said the rest was in the figgy duff! I told him to serve it out in the middle; he just looked astonished but they got on with it. I stood on top and watched him setting out the dixies and soldiers of both sides lined up with their mess tins. If I say that I couldn't believe my eyes, that is no exaggeration.

In the afternoon I searched out von Marburg and asked him what he intended to do. He said that he had organised a burial party for any dead Germans lying out in nml and suggested we did too. So just before dusk we had a kind of joint funeral service with the

German chaplain for about twenty men who had been killed and were interred in the middle of nml. He was Catholic but it made no difference and we all stood lined up on both sides of the graves while the priest said his service in German. We had crosses made from ration boxes but the Germans actually had smart official ones. I told von M that we would go back our lines at dusk but would not fire. He agreed and we sent the men back, then saluted, shook hands and I walked slowly back to our lines.

I cannot believe what has happened today. What it means for the war I can only guess.

26 December 1914.(Written on the 27th)
My thoughts on what happened on Xmas day have been shaken. Not a shot was fired all day yesterday and some of the soldiers said to me that maybe it meant the war was over. However we were relieved at dusk (much to our surprise as we expected another five days in the line) by a bn of the Camerons from another brigade. They were not happy as they had only come out of the line 72 hours before and had been told they would get 3 weeks rest. Marched back to Dikkebus and back into tents. All very odd.

The rumour mill is working overtime tonight. CSM told me that he had heard that pretty well the whole BEF had downed tools on Xmas day and fraternised with the Germans! Amazing.

28 December 1914.
Warned for an inspection tomorrow by no less than
GOC 2 Corps; sir Horace Smith-Dorrien, and ex-
Forester himself. Heavy guns!

29 December 1914
Battalion was inspected by General Smith-Dorrien,
commanding 2 Corps. Very formal! He walked along
the ranks on foot, talked to the soldiers and generally
sniffed around far more than I expected. He asked me
all kinds of questions, about how was morale in the
company, what had happened on Christmas Day, etc.
Told him the truth and he seemed to understand. He
was accompanied by a captain on the staff who took
down my answers in a notebook, which I didn't much
care for. Stopped at Kearey (naturally) and asked him
about his scarred cheek, which I have to admit, is
pretty striking. Kearey gave him a colourful account
of the incident and Major Stockton - who is now an
acting Lt. Col. – fixed me with a stare and added that
Kearey was in for a DCM. Old Smith-Dorrien cried,
'Capital! Capital!' and smote Kearey cheerfully on
the arm before proceeding down the ranks.

When he had finished he addressed the troops.
Told us that as an old Forester himself he was
delighted with our turnout and bearing. Warned us
that we were in for a long war but absolute confidence
of victory. Usual tripe. Then he said that "the
unfortunate events of Christmas day must never be
repeated" and dismissed us. All very odd.

Colonel Stockton wouldn't be drawn on the subject of Xmas Day afterwards, nor would Johnny Wybergh. It's like it never happened, although I heard from a Worcesters captain in the mess tent afterwards that a Scots Guards company commander is to be court martialled for allowing his men to fraternise with the Germans on Christmas Day. Don't know if it is true or not. Can't be any more guilty than I am or the other company commanders!

CHAPTER 12

HOME LEAVE, JANUARY 1915

Thumbing through Grandpa Gunn's diaries I have been struck by how his handwriting varies. At times of great pressure it is a bit erratic and slopes forward, but when he is more composed and has more time, it is more vertical. For example, when writing about the trench raid back in the first week of December 1914 it is obviously very rushed, but when he later talks of the court martial of the soldier who deliberately shot himself in the hand it is much more measured and composed.

These examples makes it plain.

The court martial of Private Barraclough seems to have moved Gunn greatly. On the one hand he sympathises with the soldier as a young, nervous lad; on the other hand, he feels that discipline must be maintained, although he is obviously shocked by the death sentence, which he clearly feels was excessive as this extract (written on 5 January 1915) makes clear:

Sjt Ruddock comes back from the Field General Court Martial of Private Barraclough back at Poperinghe with a long face. Apparently Barraclough was found guilty and sentenced to death. While I am not surprised by the verdict, the sentence seems far too heavy. Ruddock said that the whole trial was incredibly slow with everything being taken down in longhand by the President of the Court, a senior major from the Glosters. Ruddock (who had been called as a witness) said that Barraclough was obviously very shaken up. He had nearly blown his left hand off and was still very pale and shaky, according to Ruddock. He told me that our M.O. Captain Dunn had been called to give evidence about the wound, and had been very damning, Ruddock said. The doc had testified that there was smoke blackening and powder round the wound, so it must have been fired at close range.

Barraclough's defence appears to have been 'he couldn't take it any more,' which cut no ice with the court as he had only been out for a few weeks and had only been in one action!

Johnny Wybergh was dragged back to act as Prisoner's Friend, much to his irritation. Told me he pleaded B's youth and shaken nerves as a mitigation plea. Much good it did him. I could tell them a thing or two about shaken nerves! Poor old Barraclough has now disappeared back down the line into some military hospital to await his fate. According to Colonel Stockton, he is unlikely to be shot and will probably end up in a military prison.

This was almost Gunn's last entry before being sent back to England for a week's leave on 14th January. The Foresters were in Corps reserve at Brandhoek, west of Ypres, and, although he did not know it at the time, Gunn had been put forward for the new medal, the Military Cross.

Gunn's account of his leave that January is very thin, with only a few lines on each day. He clearly went to Oxshott in Surrey by train, arriving home on the same day he sailed from France. He talks very little of his 'sweetheart', Dorothy, and is clearly vexed by a suggestion that he goes north to Nottingham to see his grandparents.

Curiously he spends his last day travelling to London a day early, where he stayed in Brown's hotel overnight before catching the leave train back to France from Victoria. He mentions an 'L', which from later entries is almost certainly a young woman called Lydia...

Gunn's leave came as a complete surprise and a shock. On the 13th of January he was told to report immediately to the Adjutant at battalion HQ, where he found a grinning Johnny Wybergh, who thrust a bunch of papers into his hand and said, 'You've got a week's leave, Tommy! Starts tomorrow, early ack emma.'

Next morning a slightly stunned Gunn made his way to the station at Poperinghe to begin the trip back to England. Hundreds of soldiers from all regiments stood around smoking and exchanging cheerful banter. An end-of-term air of excitement hung over the crowd. A large group of officers stood apart, while harassed transport officers tried to check leave papers as the old French locomotive slowly clanked to a stop amid billowing clouds of steam in the cold yellow winter sun. Looking out of the window from the officers' carriage, Gunn stared silently as the winter landscape rolled past. A week's leave!

As if in a daze, he joined the leave boat at Boulogne and, escorted by a grey Royal Navy destroyer, stood on deck listening to the wheeling gulls as the cold, oily calm waters of the Channel slid by beneath him. Life passed in a dream-like, unreal daze. He could hardly believe it.

Michael Phillips, a captain in the Lancashire Fusiliers whom he had met on a pre-war course, recognised him and walked across to suggest they have lunch together. They had both been at the School of Musketry in Hythe and had enjoyed some jolly evenings in the past. He was going back on leave too.

Despite this, the talk was slightly stilted at first. Both men were quiet and withdrawn, unable to believe that they really were away from the fighting and the danger. Both had been through similar experiences in the trenches. Phillips had been out since Le Cateau in August and, like Gunn, was obviously shaken by the sights he had seen; perhaps more so.

He told Gunn of a shell which had landed on his company's headquarters dugout the week before, killing all the officers, who had been assembled for an orders group. 'I only missed it because I was coming down the communication trench with the orders from battalion HQ' he said. He drained and immediately refilled his wine glass. Gunn noticed that his friend's hands were shaking slightly. 'Four of them. And the serjeant major. We had to dig him out. But he'd suffocated by then.' He looked at Gunn. 'I was the only officer left in the company, then. Poor buggers.' His voice was slightly shrill. 'Another ten yards and I'd have been one of them too. All my company officers. Except me.' He waved for another bottle of wine.

Of the 30-odd officers who had come out with the Second Lancashires with the BEF, only six originals were left with the battalion, according to Phillips. Gunn poured himself another glass of red wine and tried to work out how many of the original Forester officers were left; after a moment's furious concentration he announced that it was ten, plus the doctor.

Both men looked at each other. 'How many soldiers?' asked Gunn.

'I can't tell you exactly,' Phillips replied. 'We mobilised back in August and were a thousand strong. Now...' He shrugged. 'Now I don't suppose we've got a third of the original battalion. If that. What about you?'

'Pretty much the same.'

The two men looked at each other. 'It can't go on like this,' said Phillips. 'We'll run out of men if there's another big battle.'

Gunn was inclined to agree. He noticed the blue rings under Phillips eyes and the slightly haunted look of his old friend as he looked away frequently and stared into space. Gunn wondered if he too was suffering from the shock that seemed to have reduced his normally cheerful chum to a withdrawn and morose silence.

At Newhaven the two rushed to share a train up to

Victoria, where they parted: Gunn for his short journey to Waterloo and Surrey; Phillips to Euston and then the London North Western railway to his people up near Oldham. They shook hands.

'I wonder if we'll ever meet again?' mused Phillips.

Gunn was shocked. 'Come on, old man! It isn't that bad, surely? Look on the bright side. You've got a week's leave and then you're staying on as adjutant to one of these new Kitchener service battalions at Preston, you told me. You'll get a good rest there, I'm sure.'

Phillips stared at him. His pale blue eyes were clouded as he stared over Gunn's shoulder. 'And then? When's the next one going to get us?'

Gunn clapped his old friend on the back. 'Cheer up, man. We've made it this far. We'll make it the rest. You'll see. Now, push off and grab a cab while you can.'

Phillips nodded slowly and, clutching his officer's valise, walked off into the smoky gloom of a London January. As he watched the departing form, Gunn wondered if his friend was all right. He had seen men shocked by their experience of war before. Still, he thought, with a decent leave and now a home posting, dear old Michael will have plenty of time to recover his nerve. The high jinks of those shared late evenings in Hythe and Folkestone hotel bars seemed an age away.

Waterloo and the line to Guildford went by in a dream. As he walked up the slope into Oxshott, Gunn took in the scene of his home village as the dusk fell and the short winter day ended. He wondered if his telegram from Newhaven had been delivered and whether his parents would be waiting for him.

As he turned the corner and trudged up the short path, the front door suddenly swung open in a blaze of light and his delighted mother greeted him with open arms. 'Taddy! Dearest Taddy! I can't believe you're really here.' She hugged him tight.

He hugged her back. 'Am I really home?'

Gunn was swept into the bosom of the family from the start. He was dumped in a chair in the drawing room in front of a roaring fire, while a new maid called Morag brought him tea. He stared up into her violet blue eyes as she said, 'Or would you prefer something stronger, sir?' From her voice she was a bit Irish, he thought. Gunn realised that in all honesty he would have preferred the *chota peg* of a stiff whisky, but opted for the tea to please his mother.

The family spaniel, Trudy, came in and, after greeting him excitedly with big licks to his face, settled down to sniffing his boots before flopping down with a contented sigh by the fire. The tea was hot and strong and Gunn half listened to his mother's chatter he luxuriated in the warmth from the fire. He tried to concentrate on what she was saying.

'...Raymond is doing very well. He's in his last year at Tonbridge. He has his exams this summer and will probably get a place at Cambridge, according to Father. However, Raymond says he's going to try and join up when he leaves in the summer. He'll be eighteen by then, of course. And your sister is away this week on some trip or other that the school has organised to Wales. Pity. I know that she would have loved to have seen you, Taddy.'

She bent down to retrieve her knitting from a bag by her chair and started clicking away with the needles. 'Father is out tending to one of the one of the labourers over at Stoke d'Abernon. Trapped his hand in the thresher, I think. He'll be back for dinner. He uses that new motor car of his now to do the patients' visits. He says it's better than all the bother of the dog cart, although that's still in out in the back in the stable with Brander.' Brander was the pony that drew their dog cart or trap.

'Now tell me about yourself; of course, we read your letters; but I just want to know how you are.' In her heart, his mother thought that Gunn looked desperately tired and not himself.

Gunn gave a very bald account of his doings since the autumn, ending with an oblique reference to shells and casualties and how lucky he had been. When he had finished his mother nodded and said, 'Yes, I can understand. We have had the same thing here too, you know, dear. Why, look at those dreadful shellings of ordinary people up in the north east. Over a hundred civilians killed when they shelled Hartlepool, according to the newspapers! It was nothing less than murder. And now your father tells me he won't be surprised if they don't try and drop shells from those great Zeppelin things. It's a disgrace. Oh, we have suffered from the war, no doubt.'

In vain Gunn tried to compare the German navy's brief snap raid to bombard Hartlepool and Scarborough with the day in, day out reality of constant shelling in the icy mud of the trenches and its steady toll of maiming and death. He felt a surge of resentment as his mother added, 'So we civilians know what this war is about, too, you know.'

Fortunately his response remained unsaid as his father came in. Dr Albert Oliver William Gunn was a tall man, with a florid face and greying hair. Despite his farm visit, he was still

wearing his GP's uniform of morning coat and striped trousers.
A slight odour of iodine or chloroform hung around him. He
greeted his wife with, 'A broken hand. Lucky to keep it. He's
at the Cottage Hospital.' Then he shook his son warmly by the
hand and asked the universal question, 'Well, well, m'boy,
good to see you. Jolly good. How long have you got?'

'Just a week, Father.'

'Good Lord! I thought you'd have longer.' He shook his
head. 'That's going to make it jolly difficult seeing your
grandparents.'

Gunn had been dreading this conversation. The Gunn
family had moved down from Nottingham to Surrey in 1903
when his father had bought the Oxshott practice. Gunn had
been 13 at the time with a half scholarship to Nottingham
High School already. As a result, he had spent the next five
years staying up in Nottingham during term, living in his
grandparents' house on Portland Road as a day boy at the
school, and enjoying his holidays at home in Oxshott with his
younger brother and sister. This week he had no wish to waste
half his leave – as he saw it – rushing up to Nottingham to see
his grandparents, much as he cared for them.

'I agree. I don't think there's going to be much time, Father.
Maybe on my next leave?'

His father pursed his lips and rubbed a hand over his
thinning hair. 'Well, you know best, Thaddeus. But they're
going to be deuced disappointed.'

He turned to his wife and pulled out his watch. 'Gone six!
Good Lord! Elizabeth, I'll just go and get washed and changed.'
He glanced at his son. 'Dinner at half past seven suit you?' He
looked at Gunn's dusty boots. 'I expect you'll be looking

forward to getting out of that army uniform for a while, eh?'

Lying back in his armchair, Gunn looked down at his boots and suddenly for a brief moment he was transported back. He remembered looking down at them when they had buried Simpson at La Bassée. He had stared hard at the boots as the soldiers had shovelled what was left of the corporal into a canvas farm sack, unable to look at a dismembered human being who was now reduced to unrecognisable chunks of meat. He remembered staring down at his boots when Doc Dunn had come in to battalion HQ after the trench raid, his white apron splashed with blood, obviously genuinely surprised to see him in the fug and lamp light of the dugout. '*Good God! I heard you had gone West …*' echoed in his mind. A vision of Doughty's sticky bayonet and the dreadful crunching noise as he pushed it into the German's skull in the dark made him shudder.

In his reverie he failed to notice the exchange of glances between his parents. His mother gave a sharp shake of her head as the older Gunn looked at her quizzically, eyebrows raised.

Gradually Thaddeus came back to reality. He was suddenly very tired. The heat of the fire and the stuffiness of the room had got to him. Wearily he stood up and said, 'I think I'll go and get washed and changed for dinner.'

He looked round the well-remembered room, with its lace covers on the back of the chairs, the brass fireguard and the aspidistra plant in a pot by the bay window. The firelight was reflecting red on the dark pictures on the walls.

His mother watched him walk out, moving like an old man. 'Your room is just as you left it, dear. There's plenty of hot water and you'll hear the dinner gong.'

Gunn clambered wearily upstairs.

His parents found him later, when he didn't come down to dinner; half undressed and sprawled on top of his bed, snoring gently. He'd pulled his boots and tunic off. His mother gently lifted an eiderdown over her sleeping son and switched the light out.

* * *

Next morning Gunn was up early. He had slept through and was slightly embarrassed. His casual civilian clothes felt strange and seemed to hang loose on him. As he drank coffee and glanced at the paper in the dining room, Mrs Gibson the cook bustled in with the breakfast dishes and gave him a warm hug. 'Why, Mister Thaddeus! I heard you were back. How are you, sir? When do you have to go back? I've done bacon and mushrooms special for you, because I know it's your favourite. Oh, it is so good to see you!'

She eyed him up and down. 'Why, you've lost weight, I do believe. Working you hard out there in France, are they?'

Gunn grinned ruefully. Emily Gibson had been with the Gunn family for over ten years. Her husband had died back in 1902, leaving her destitute. Doctor Gunn had offered her the post of cook to the household, as he felt that somehow he should have done more to save a very sick Jack Gibson; but the growth in the jobbing carpenter's lung had been inoperable. A motherly fifty-something, Mrs Gibson now looked on the Gunns as her family. She had no children of her own and had watched the children grow up.

As Gunn helped himself to mushrooms, bacon and eggs, she strode across to the brass gong in the hall and gave it a couple a healthy bongs. Doctor Gunn appeared from the morning room, in a cardigan over his white shirt and tie. *The Times* hung from his fingers. 'Ah, up and about, I see. Good man! I expect you're used to rising early in the army?'

For the second time since his homecoming, Gunn felt a twinge of unease. Didn't these civilians, even his family, warm, decent, comfortable, above all, *safe*, understand what it was like? Didn't they realise what they were suffering at the front? He held his tongue.

Doctor Gunn helped himself to a pair of kippers and started eviscerating their bones with surgical skill.

'So what's the plan today? And this week? I expect you'll be wanting to see Dorothy? I'll let old Carmichael know you're really back. I could even drive you over to Cobham, you know. That motor car has made a real difference to getting around the practice. Morris Oxford. New machine. Ten horse power. Cost me nearly £200 - imagine! But I can drive it myself, it's reliable and out on the old Portsmouth road she'll reach nearly fifty miles an hour. Best buy I ever made.' He poured himself a second cup of tea.

Mrs Gunn appeared, wearing a housecoat. She kissed Thaddeus absently on the head and rang for more toast. 'How are you, Taddy? We let you sleep through. You were exhausted. What are your plans?'

Gunn nodded. 'Thank you, Mother. Well, today's Friday. I've got to go back for next Thursday, that's the 21st.'

Gunn thought about what he really wanted to do on his

leave. He had been so surprised by getting leave in the first place that he hadn't really considered how to spend his time. He just knew that he didn't want to spend two days travelling up to Nottingham.

'I suppose I'll stay in the village today. Just relax, maybe a walk on the Common. Tomorrow's Saturday, so I might pop into Esher, have a look around.'

'And Sunday's church,' reminded his mother. 'Matins, ten thirty.'

'We could fix lunch with the Carmichaels for Sunday, you know,' added Doctor Gunn. 'They all want to see you.'

'That's that, then,' said Gunn. 'I'm just happy to be back.'

'Good man,' his father said, getting up and carefully folding his napkin to put it into his silver ring. 'I'll see what the nine o'clock surgery is like and then I'll telephone Carmichael to see what we can fix up for Sunday.' He looked at his wife munching her toast. 'I'll be in the surgery if you need me, dear. Thaddeus; you just relax and enjoy yourself. Get some fresh air. Might even take a wander into the Victoria, this evening, eh? Lots of folk will want to talk to you, I'm sure. It's all round the village.'

Gunn's day passed quietly. He spent the morning chatting to his mother, answering increasingly irritating questions. Elizabeth Gunn seemed genuinely puzzled that he had been spending most of his time living in a cold, cramped muddy cave in the ground. The realities of soldiering on the Western Front seemed beyond her.

'But can't they give you tents, dear?' she said at one point. Keeping his patience with some difficulty, Gunn pointed out that the Germans were only a few hundred yards away, trying to kill him and living in equally primitive conditions.

After a lunch of mutton chops he said he would go for a walk on the Common, just to escape from the vapid questions. Wrapped up warm against the January cold, he wandered up the sandy incline and under a cold grey sky, roamed the pine trees and the woods that he remembered from his youth. Deep in the wood, he sat on the cold earth for a while and watched a red squirrel searching for its long buried nuts. He remained totally still as the squirrel cocked its head on one side, inspecting him suspiciously before digging for what looked like a muddy acorn, which it stripped and nibbled furiously.

Only when it had finished did he dare to move. The squirrel shot up a tree to look down at him, its little face chattering fiercely in indignation. He waved his walking stick at the branch and the squirrel shot away up the trunk. The last he saw was its red-ochre tail flicking round a branch.

Cold and somehow saddened by the encounter, he retraced his steps towards the village and home. As he crossed the railway bridge he was greeted by a village woman he knew, laden with shopping from London. 'Hello Mr Gunn,' she said. 'Heard you were back. How's life in France?' Then she scurried away. Gunn suddenly realised that he felt lonely here, in his old home village. His friends were out in France; here, he had nothing to do and no one seemed to understand. He shook his head and plodded home.

He was greeted with tea and a pile of post, which his mother said that she hadn't bothered to send it all on as "it was mainly bank statements and bills." He opened the envelopes one by one. There were the usual bleats of dismay from his London tailor, who received a regular £4 a month by standing order anyway, so he ignored those.

His bank statements came as a shock. The Army agents had been receiving his monthly pay since August. At 8/6 a day, and then 12/6 a day after he had taken over the company, he was staggered to discover that he had no less than £112 and eight shillings in his account. His cheques with the Field Cashier in France had been deducted - he checked. He was rich! Well, better off than serving in the peacetime regiment, anyway.

Sitting back and stroking Trudy's silken head, he smiled. 'Good news, dear?' enquired his mother.

'It's just I've done rather well at the bank. Can't spend all that much money out in France,' he explained. He yawned and stretched. 'I think I'll go into Esher tomorrow. Have a mooch around. Maybe a spot of lunch.'

His mother did something complicated with her knitting. 'That's nice, dear. You need to get out and relax. And Father tells me that he has telephoned Mr Carmichael and we're all going over to Cobham for lunch on Sunday. He's determined to take us all for a spin in that new motor of his. So you'll be able to see Dorothy.'

Feeling slightly cheered by the news of his bank account, Gunn walked down to the Victoria at six o'clock, promising to be back for seven thirty. He arrived at the pub, all red brick and with a blazing coal fire, to find that there were half a dozen villagers in the saloon bar already. A more sensitive man than Gunn might have wondered why they were all there so early in the evening. It never occurred to him that they were waiting to see him and pump him for news of the war.

Old Billings, the City lawyer who, rumour had it, was the

richest man in the village, greeted him warmly, offering a drink. Gunn opted for wine, at which Thomas Skill, the local bank manager, nodded sagely, 'Ah, yes. Wine. I expect you'll be drinking a lot of that out in France, Gunn.'

As he sipped his wine and lit a cigar, Gunn realised from the line of conversation that these middle-aged men were desperate for information from France. The British papers were painfully thin on news from the Front and the BEF. These men were starved of real news. He tried to answer their questions, only to discover that they hadn't the slightest comprehension of what was really going on.

At one point Billings said, 'So you say that lots of buildings have been knocked down and destroyed?' He took a pull at his gin. 'That's bad. Very bad. So how do the Frenchies sort out their commercial claims for compensation? Can they go to law?'

Gunn looked at him blankly. 'I haven't the faintest idea. It's a war. There are no lawyers. There is no compensation.'

He took refuge in wine, while Billings' forehead knotted in sheer astonishment. 'So what's happened to all these buildings? And the people, naturally?' he added as a commercial lawyer's afterthought.

Gunn smiled grimly. 'The buildings are flattened. Half of Northern France is occupied by the Huns. As for the people, mostly they've run away. Refugees. Just like the Belgians.'

Matthew Billings, successful commercial lawyer in the City of London, shook his head with disbelief as he tried to visualise a world in which there were no lawyers and no possibility of claiming for damage. 'It's barbarous!' he concluded.

'No; Mr Billings: it's war,' said Gunn quietly. He leaned back and listened to their talk, realising that there was no way he could ever bring the reality of the trenches home to these people. A tall and thin young man in a startling check suit, whom he didn't recognise, was hovering on the edge of the group, listening intently. Gunn wondered why he wasn't in the army.

'So, how many Germans have you killed?' asked the stranger.

Gunn was astonished at the question. 'I've no idea.' A flash of anger at the stupid civilian gripped him. 'At least one.'

'Good heavens,' said the young man, shocked. 'Whatever happened?'

'I stabbed him in the head with a bayonet,' said Gunn with sudden savagery. 'Right through the brain. In the dark.'

The young man recoiled and someone said, 'Good God!' Billings looked at him open-mouthed. 'But as an officer… I mean…'

Gunn called for another glass of wine. 'It was on a trench raid. In the dark. In a shell hole. He fell in and we killed him.' He looked round the group. 'We lost ten men that night. Some to our own shells falling short. Some blown to bits'

He noticed the young man had turned a little pale. Gunn stared hard at him. 'That's why we need every able-bodied man at the Front. I've lost too many of my friends already.' He savoured his second glass of red wine. The first had been a bit cold and sour. Now it had warmed and breathed a little, it was better. He expected that old Charlie Fletcher the landlord had opened the bottle specially for him. There wasn't much call for claret in the Victoria, even in the saloon bar.

Gunn eyed his circle of listeners with a calculating eye. 'This war is going to last a long time, I think. We'll need every man we can get before it's over.' They looked shocked. The young man looked alarmed, finished his drink quickly and slid out. The others began talking among themselves.

Gunn's gaze strayed to a mirror, and he suddenly realised he could see into the public bar next door. In the glass he saw Farmer Denks watching his reflection back. He excused himself and walked through to the Public. The spit and sawdust bar was fairly full already, mostly with farm workers and some of the local labourers. He recognised Mike Green, the blacksmith's burly son, clutching a pint pot of stout. From his flushed face Gunn thought that it probably wasn't his first.

He went up to Denks and shook his hand. 'Mr Denks. A pleasure to see you. I hear your boys joined up?'

Denks nodded cheerfully. 'Right enough, Mr Gunn. All three of the buggers, damn them. All gone to the East Surreys. Some Service Battalion or other. Makes working the farm a bit difficult, I can tell you.' He eyed Gunn up and down. 'And how about you, sir? You're looking fit, if I may say so.'

Gunn grinned. He liked old Denks, who'd belted him years before when he'd caught him sliding down on of his haystacks during the school holidays. 'It's the outdoor life, Mr Denks, living in the fields. Bit like working on the land, I daresay?'

Denks remembered the Boer War; his brother had died out in South Africa with the Imperial Yeomanry. Fever. He grunted; 'Right enough. Except some bugger's trying to kill you.'

Gunn nodded. Mike Green moved in waving his beer pot, and slopping a little in the process. 'So what's it like out there, then?'

Gunn looked around and saw the same hungry faces he had seen among the saloon bar's inhabitants, desperate for real news. He thought hard about his reply. These were after all young men, hardened by a working life in the fields.

He took a mouthful of wine. 'Well, I'll be honest with you boys, it's hard. We're cold, we're wet, the mud and the rain are dreadful, and the grub isn't even as good as Charlie Fletcher's bread and cheese here in the Victoria. And it's dangerous. Damn dangerous. My regiment has lost a lot of good men since we went to France. That's what it's like, if I'm honest. It's man's work out there.'

They were hanging on his every word.

'But we'll win. Even if it takes another year, we'll win.' No great orator, Gunn stopped abruptly. Someone slapped him on the back.

'That's the spirit, sir,' called another voice. 'Here, get Mr Gunn another drink,' said another.

Gunn looked at his watch and remembered that it was nearly time for dinner. With a grim, 'Gentlemen, Thank you, but no. It has been a pleasure. The dinner gong calls,' he walked out.

Next morning he took the 11.27 train to Esher, determined to get some time on his own. Gunn was not an introspective man – which regular army officer in autumn 1914 could afford to be? However, his experiences thus far on leave had shaken him. His views on the war were clearly light years removed from the general view of the British public, and that troubled him.

Thaddeus Gunn was not a man given to laugh at Britain

or himself; but when a smartly-dressed young woman handed him a white feather as he emerged from the Bear in the High Street in his tweed suit after a good lunch, he burst out laughing.

'What's the matter?' she cried. 'It's no laughing matter. A strong, fit young man like you? You should be ashamed of yourself. Why aren't you in the Army. Don't you know your duty? Where's your pride? Where's your manhood?'

A decent steak, a half bottle of good claret and a large cognac had reduced Gunn to something approaching acceptance of what was now an alien world. He burst out:

'You stupid woman! You're one of those Suffragettes, I'll wager.'

'I am,' she responded proudly. 'And we believe that every man must do his duty.'

Gunn eyed her up and down. She was a good looking sort, he decided, despite the fanatic's gleam in her eye.

Drink, irritation and frustration fuelled his reply. 'You're a very stupid woman; you're a fool. You haven't the faintest idea what you are asking.' He noticed some pedestrians stopped on the pavement, listening. 'Let me tell you, Madam, I am a serving officer in the Sherwood Foresters, on a week's leave from the trenches in France. I have seen my friends killed, and my men butchered in the past few months. You know nothing. NOTHING! Only when I see you and your womankind in the front line ready to die, will I listen to you and your silly entreaties. You haven't the faintest idea of what this war is really like.'

The woman recoiled as if struck. He moved towards her. 'So get out of my way, you stupid ... bitch!'

People stopped walking past and turned to listen. The woman was appalled. 'What did you call me? How dare you? You call yourself a British army officer? You call yourself a gentleman?'

'Indeed I am, Madam,' said Gunn, now relaxed and back in control. 'Captain Gunn of Four Foresters.' He felt better for his outburst. 'A regular officer. And I know what this war is all about because I have been in France.'

She stood shocked, her hand to her mouth. 'Which you, with respect, do not. Have you ever been to France? Have you?'

She shook her head, frightened.

'Quite. No. So you have not the faintest idea about this war. You know nothing about the army. And yet you have the temerity to wander the streets handing out white feathers to regular army officers in civilian clothes? For shame!'

He towered over her. 'Now, if you want to do something really useful, then may I suggest that you go and enrol as a nurse, instead of harassing real soldiers who have seen real fighting? After all, there are plenty of wounded soldiers who badly need your help.'

There was a long silence. He tipped his hat. 'That's more important than walking the streets handing out white feathers to complete strangers, is it not? Now, I am sure we all have better things to do. And a very good day to you, Madam,' and walked off.

She stared after him, open-mouthed.

A bystander said, 'Blimey. That's told her.' Someone gave a faint cheer. Walking away, Gunn grinned. Suddenly, he felt much better.

The rest of his leave passed quickly. The trip out to Cobham next day in his father's beloved Morris was just as he had expected. Dorothy greeted him coolly and allowed him to peck her chastely-upturned cheek. In her long pale blue dress with its severe collar she had obviously made an effort to look nice for his visit. He caught her hazel eyes and she smiled as he complimented her on her looks. Although no striking beauty, Dorothy Carmichael was still considered quite a catch by the Cobham gentry. Her somewhat prominent nose was easily ignored as he took in her English rose complexion and long chestnut hair. At twenty-three Dorothy was definitely expecting to be married soon – an expectation heartily shared by her parents.

Over the grilled sardines, Gunn was once again quizzed about what it was really like in France and, rather to his own surprise, he found himself becoming monosyllabic and understating the true facts. That puzzled him, as deep down Gunn really wanted to tell the truth to the little group round the table and explain to them what life was really like in the trenches; it was just that he was beginning to realise that there wasn't any point. Even if he did tell them, they wouldn't understand. Worse, he thought as he accepted a second helping of the Carmichaels' excellent roast beef, these nice, decent folk *couldn't* understand what it was like. So he held his tongue and let the conversation roam to other areas.

Old Carmichael had served a glass of white wine with the sardines and Gunn listened to him apologising that it wasn't Hock, but German wines were quite clearly unacceptable, nowadays. Everyone agreed. Gunn, remembering the

Christmas Day Truce, was going to ask if German Christmas Carols were now beyond the pale as well; but looking round the table thought better of it. He wondered idly if Mozart and Bach were now banned too. Was everything German bad now? And what about Handel? He came from Germany. Or did both sides play his music still?

After selecting the apple pie instead of the rice pudding, all Gunn wanted to do was doze off in an armchair by the fire. But Mrs Carmichael, a tall, rather assertive woman with decided ideas about her daughter's future, had other ideas and said brightly, 'Why don't you two young people go for a nice walk? I'm sure you can find lots to talk about.'

So Gunn, somewhat to his irritation, found himself well muffled up and strolling through the icy streets of Cobham on a cold January afternoon. Dorothy took his arm as he tried to listen to her chattering on about her own interests and the doings of rural Surrey. Their breath steamed in the freezing air as they wandered idly down towards the River Mole and the old water mill. There were few other walkers out on such a cold, bleak afternoon. She was talking about weddings, he suddenly realised with a jolt of alarm.

'...so many people are getting married these days before their man goes off to the war. Ever so many. The newspapers are full of weddings, you know.' She stopped and looked at him. He saw a flash of calculation in her eye. 'How long have we known each other for, Taddy?'

'Oh, ages...' he began.

'Ever since you went off to Sandhurst. That's when we really met.' Gunn had gone to Sandhurst in 1910, some four years before. Dorothy fixed him with a determined look on her face. 'It's a long time for us to have known each other. Isn't it, don't you think?'

Well aware of where this conversation was heading, an increasingly alarmed Gunn tried to deflect her. 'Quite. Absolutely. And we're jolly good friends still, aren't we?'

That was a mistake. She pounced on it and squeezed his arm. 'You're right. We are. In fact, I think we're really rather close, don't you?'

Gunn didn't - but dare not say it. He was quite convinced by now that Dorothy Carmichael was trying to manoeuvre him into proposing to her. That was clearly what was behind the walk. Suddenly he remembered the exchange of glances between mother and daughter as the left the Carmichael's house. And of one thing Gunn was sure; he may have had ideas about his supposed sweetheart Dorothy Carmichael in the past, but he had no intention of getting married to anyone right now, least of all Dorothy Carmichael, however much her fond Mama liked the idea and however 'satisfactory' it might be for the two families. His soul rebelled against the whole idea.

He tried to let her down gently. He took his arm away from her and turned to face her. 'I've got something to tell you, Dorothy. Something important,' he began. He tugged at his moustache.

She stared up at him expectantly, eyes bright with excitement.

He cleared his throat. 'Y'see, this war is going to go on for some time. After what I've seen, I'm absolutely convinced of that. And that means that this is no time for anyone to, well, you know, get serious or get engaged or anything like that.'

She looked shocked.

He pressed on hurriedly, 'Wouldn't be fair. I mean a chap's away at the Front all the time; could get hurt; wounded. Killed even.' Her eyes widened with surprise. 'No, it's not on. Wouldn't be right. Not fair on the lady. Sure you agree, Dorothy. Sure you understand. Not with the war on.' He tugged at his moustache again. 'Better wait for happier times before coming to any arrangements, yes?'

She sniffed, glared at him and turned for home. He could see that she was anything but understanding, and this was confirmed by her stiff back and silence all the way back to the house. For once Gunn's social antennae were finely tuned and he caught the enquiring look that passed between mother and daughter as they went back into the house, followed by the infinitesimal shake of Dorothy's head. He noted the mother's pursed lips as they said farewell and the slight coolness that had fallen over the Carmichaels.

On the way back, Dr Gunn said that he thought that Mrs Carmichael seemed 'a bit out of sorts' as they had left. Gunn's mother agreed and asked her son if he and Dorothy had fallen out on their walk. 'Not at all,' said Gunn, adding enigmatically, 'I just think things didn't quite turn out as she expected.'

Old Doctor Gunn grinned to himself. He knew his eldest son. 'Or her mother, either.' It was a statement, not a question. 'Oh well, never mind,' he added philosophically. 'It was a good lunch.' They finished the journey to Oxshott in silence.

On Monday Gunn announced that he would be leaving on Wednesday, explaining that the leave train left early from Victoria for Folkestone and he needed to be in London overnight. His mother was upset, but she could see that Gunn was bored by Oxshott and wanted a night on his own in London.

So on Wednesday afternoon he caught the train up to Waterloo and, taking comfort from his well-stocked bank account, decided to splash out and book in at Brown's hotel in Mayfair. He was greeted by a rather supercilious hall porter who looked Gunn's captain's uniform up and down and, with many faintly-dropped aitches, asked him if he minded waiting a moment. Gunn did rather mind and was just about to say so when the flunkey added, 'You see, Queen Elisabeth will be coming aht in a moment, sir.'

'Queen Elisabeth?' Startled, Gunn stood on the pavement as a gaggle of Belgian officers and courtiers erupted from the hotel doors, followed by a small, smartly-dressed, rather horse-faced woman. He saluted as the party piled into glossy motor cars and drove off. The doorman watched them go, observing, 'For a German she hain't so bad. Considering.'

'German?'

'Yus. Queen Elisabeth. Princess of Bavaria as was. Married the Belgian Crahn Prince before the war. So now she's the Belgians' Queen. German all right. No doubt abaht it. Tricky eh, sir? German, see? She lives 'ere now.'

Head reeling, Gunn booked in. Brown's Hotel was full of surprises.

He got a bigger surprise in the bar before dinner. Half a dozen well-dressed and attractive young women were packed at the bar, laughing and joking with a couple of tweed-suited older men who seemed to be in charge. There were no other uniforms in the bar and one of the girls turned to Gunn with a smile and a cheer. 'Hurray! At last!' she exclaimed. 'A soldier.'

A faint cheer went up and one of the girls broke into, 'Oh we don't want to lose you, but we think you ought to go...' in a surprisingly good voice. To Gunn's embarrassment the others all joined in the song. When they had finished there was a cheer. Gunn raised his glass and said, 'But I've been already!' which raised a delighted laugh.

One of the men said, 'Have a drink with me, lad. What'll you have?' Baffled by the group, Gunn accepted another glass of gin and bitters and turned to eye the girls. It turned out that they were part of the chorus from one of the West End theatres. They crowded round him, laughing and joking and plied him with questions about what it was like in France.

They were pretty, they were lively and articulate, and they were quite unlike any women Gunn had met before; bolder and more flirtatious. 'Forward,' his mother would call them. One in particular held Gunn's gaze for a fraction longer than was seemly. She was a little older than the others, petite with a good figure, and with violet blue eyes below a mass of fair hair piled high. In a lull in the conversation Gunn questioned her. It turned out that her name was Lydia, she sang contralto and they were all in a show at the Haymarket. The two men were their chaperones from the theatre, where they had to be off in twenty minutes to get ready for the performance.

'Why don't you come?' said Charley, the older of the men. 'You're very welcome, young man. Anything for one of our returning heroes, eh?'

The girls crowded round. 'Oooh, yes, do come,' they

protested. Lydia plucked his sleeve and fluttered her eyelashes. 'You must come. Otherwise we won't have an audience, will we ladies?' They squealed agreement. Laughing, Gunn agreed.

The show turned out to be one of the new-fangled revues. Gunn was given a free seat in the stalls. He spotted Lydia immediately as the girls came onto the stage dressed as soldiers in khaki for a big number. To his surprise he enjoyed the show. All thoughts of France, the Regiment and going back to the trenches vanished as the evening wore on. After the show he was invited backstage to meet the whole cast. To his surprise, several other uniformed officers were there and they discussed the show affably over glasses of champagne as the girls disappeared to wipe off their make-up.

Most of the cast drifted home eventually with cheerful 'goodnights' and a few over-blown stagey kisses. At half past eleven Lydia re-appeared. Without her stage make up and dressed in a deep blue dress she looked stunning - but older. She seized a glass of champagne and drained it before grabbing another. As she sipped it slowly, her eyes locked on his as she began to question him. The crowd drifted slowly away as people broke up and went home. The pair were still talking in a corner as the room emptied and midnight approached, and a stage hand or porter appeared, explaining that he had to lock up.

Arm in arm, the pair walked out of the stage door and into the cold night air.

'Where do you live?' asked Gunn.

'Chelsea. But I'm not in a rush. What about you?'

Gunn shrugged. 'Brown's Hotel for tonight. Back to France in the morning'

She locked her fingers in his. 'Would you like me to join you for a last drink?'

Gunn looked at her, astonished. 'Don't you have to get home?'

'I can do what I like,' was the even more astonishing reply.

Gunn hailed a passing cab, his brain in a whirl. Sitting alongside her he could smell make-up and female sweat. It was exciting, and he could feel the warmth of her body. He realised that she was staring up at him. In the gloom of the cab she was beautiful and enticing. He felt himself stirring.

'Kiss me, Tommy,' she said, wrapping a gentle arm around his neck. Without a second thought he bent down and kissed her warm, wet lips. By the time the cab arrived at Brown's, passion had them both in thrall. His hand had stroked her breast and she had clutched it to her and moaned softly as she kissed him back hard.

At the hotel, the cabby winked at him conspiratorially as Gunn over-tipped him wildly and then plunged through the hotel doors into a dark and empty lobby. A sleepy night porter handed him the key to his room, and then they were upstairs.

Gunn never remembered going upstairs and hardly remembered the rush to hurl off their clothes as they plunged into each other. After two years in India, Gunn was certainly no stranger to sex, but Lydia's passion was outside his experience of flexible Indian *houris* and the occasional bored wife of a colleague who was absent in the hills. Such cantonment affairs were not uncommon, but they were pointedly ignored in the hothouse life of the Edwardian Raj. An officer could lose his career if the truth came out, let alone the shame for the wife. But this woman was different.

At one point during the night, as Lydia clambered on top of him and gently slid him inside her, he laughed.

'What's the matter, dear?' Lydia whispered.

'Nothing, my love. Nothing.' The truth was, he was suddenly visualising the chaste and manipulative Dorothy Carmichael. Making love like this to Dorothy? The idea was ridiculous. He pressed deep inside Lydia and burst into real laughter. She wriggled deep onto him and demanded, 'What? What?'

'Nothing. I was just thinking. I am so lucky. You are wonderful.' He rolled her onto her back. 'I can't think of a better way of spending my leave. I just wish that I wasn't going back tomorrow. I think I love...'

She pressed her hand to his mouth. Her fingers smelled of sex. 'Shh. Next time. We'll see. Will you write to me?'

'Of course I will.' He began to move more quickly. 'And you?'

'Oh yes, said Lydia, climbing her own mountain of ecstatic release. 'Oh yes.'

The cold light of morning for once did not bring disillusion. Propped on one elbow Gunn looked at the sleeping Lydia, without make up and snoring gently, her fair hair in disarray on the pillow, her heavy breasts hung down sideways. She was definitely older, he decided, but she seemed strangely vulnerable lying there.

When she woke she did so with a start, and he saw the guilty shadow in her eyes as she remembered the night before. He kissed her gently.

'Hello. Good morning. Are you all right?'

She grunted sleepily and mumbled something in reply.

He slapped her bare bottom gently. 'It's gone seven, Lydia, and I have to catch the ten o'clock train at Victoria.'

They parted discreetly enough outside the hotel. He had given her his card and a sheet torn from his Field Service notebook with his full regimental details and address in France written out. Lydia promised to write - and obviously meant it.

'Will you come back to me?' she begged as he tore himself away to grab a passing cab. He turned back to kiss her in the street, bold as brass, surprised at his flaunting of convention. 'Oh yes, Lydia. I'll be back. And we will stay in touch, believe me.'

Weeping slightly, she kissed him again and he waved back at her retreating form all the way down the road until the cab turned out of Albemarle Street.

'Going back from leave, sir?' enquired the cabby.

'Yes,' replied Gunn shortly.

'Well, you come back safe and sound, sir, because your fiancée looked a very nice young lady, if I may say so. I was in South Africa, you know and it's always good to have a nice lady to come home to when you're a long way away, that I can tell you.'

Gunn was floored. He didn't know whether to tell the cabby to mind his own damned business or to laugh. His fiancée? He had only just managed to escape from the clutches of Miss Dorothy Carmichael and here he was being married off by a London cabby to a showgirl he'd only just met. He started laughing.

'Not often I get young gentlemen laughing going back to France, sir,' said the puzzled cabby as he dropped him off at Victoria amid the bustle of soldiers returning from leave. Gunn tipped him handsomely, to which the surprised cabby exclaimed, 'Blimey, Guv'nor, that's generous!' He touched his cap. 'Thank you very much, sir.'

'Not at all,' said Gunn airily. 'You've just given me a very good idea.' And she's called Lydia, he muttered to himself.

He swung into the station whistling cheerfully and acknowledging the salutes of a couple of passing soldiers going the other way. To their surprise he called after them, 'Enjoy your leave, boys!'

As Thaddeus Gunn swung into the carriage he realised that, for the first time in his life, he was in love. Nineteen fifteen promised to be an exciting year – if he survived.

The end

Printed in Great Britain
by Amazon.co.uk, Ltd.,
Marston Gate.